A KIND OF LOVING

The lovely lines of a dhow as she lay at anchor off Oman were to have a dramatic effect on the lives of four people. First, the shipbuilding brothers, Christian and Benedict, were inspired to take their skills to Oman and construct a dhow themselves. Then there was Randal, who had a very special reason for the vessel to be built with all possible haste. Finally, there was Belinda who fell passionately in love with Benedict — but heartbreak and disaster would strike before true love could win through.

Books by I. M. Fresson
in the Linford Romance Library:

NO DANGEROUS RIVAL
THE CARING HEART
THE QUALITIES OF LOVE

I. M. FRESSON

A KIND OF LOVING

Complete and Unabridged

LINFORD
Leicester

First published in Great Britain in 1994 by
Robert Hale Limited
London

First Linford Edition
published 1996
by arrangement with
Robert Hale Limited
London

British Library CIP Data

Fresson, I. M. (Iris Muriel), *1902 –*
A kind of loving.—Large print ed.—
Linford romance library
1. English fiction—20th century
I. Title II. Series
823.9'14 [F]

LINCOLNSHIRE
COUNTY COUNCIL

ISBN 0–7089–7896–7

Published by
F. A. Thorpe (Publishing) Ltd.
Anstey, Leicestershire

Set by Words & Graphics Ltd.
Anstey, Leicestershire
Printed and bound in Great Britain by
T. J. Press (Padstow) Ltd., Padstow, Cornwall

This book is printed on acid-free paper

1

"SO — that's a dhow." Christian stared at the lovely ship lying motionless in the sunlit bay.

"Rather different from the ships you design in England," Richard said smiling. "They are actually built on the sands here — as they have been for generations. Same families, same tools, the only change, that they now are motorized to make them competitive."

It was Christian's first visit to Oman, his first sight of a dhow and Richard was amused by his enthusiasm. The house was close to the shore and when they returned to it Christian began asking questions. "What do the dhows do? Where do they sail?"

"They still follow the old trading routes as they did centuries ago."

Christian was thoughtful as Richard mixed drinks. "Could one of these

1

ships be adapted for holiday cruises? Is that an original idea?"

Surprised, Richard agreed that it would be. "Take a bit of planning — cost a lot. Why — would you be interested?"

"Our boatbuilding is slack because of the recession. We need a jolt. This might be it. Catch the interest of the people who can afford that kind of holiday."

Richard said thoughtfully, "A cruise visiting the ports along the old spice routes — yes — I think it's an idea." He broke off at the sound of a car. "Here's Belinda. You remember her? It's a long time since you met."

"Of course I remember — your sister — short red hair, green eyes, cheeky. Always interfering with our cricket."

"Auburn surely, and my cricket wasn't too bad considering I was not often allowed to play."

She came into the room smiling. "That was a long time ago, there's been a lot of growing since then."

"I can see that," Christian said, considering her.

These three had known each other since childhood with gaps in between and now they caught up on news over drinks while Richard told Belinda of Christian's idea. "Would it be possible?" she wanted to know and Richard said, "Randal Kent will know. I'll ask him in for a drink." He turned to Christian. "He runs an import/export business. His opinion would be useful."

Belinda frowned. "Must you bring him into it? I can't stand the man."

"I can't imagine why," Richard said. "Anyway, there is no harm in asking his opinion."

And Christian was able to form his own opinion the next evening when Randal Kent arrived. Watching him as he talked, he thought most women would find him attractive and Belinda hard to please.

Kent listened quietly while Christian explained and, when he finished, sat for a few minutes looking down at the drink in his hand, then, with a brilliant smile, said, "A splendid idea. I might be interested in the export angle myself. Now tell me what you need to know."

During the next hour, it became clear that Randal knew his subject. Finally he said, "I'll talk to the boat-builders on the shore — especially to Hassan the head man." He stood up. "I'll find out all I can and let you know before you return to England. Don't forget I might be interested if anything comes of this."

Although excited, Christian was aware of being hustled, and said, "In any case, I can't make any decision without consulting my brother."

Randal said, "I didn't know that you had a brother."

"We are partners — boat-builders. We run the business together."

"Is he likely to take this seriously?"

"Certainly, and if he is impressed he will want to come out and see for himself."

Later, Christian went down to the

shore to meet the Omani Randal had mentioned, finding him, as Randal had promised, intelligent and helpful. Two days later, Christian was back in England, talking and explaining to Benedict all that he had in mind, showing him the sketch plans he had made, hoping to engage his enthusiasm for what must sound a slightly mad proposal. But it was not too long before Benedict became interested enough to agree that the subject should have further study.

"At least this Kent fellow sounds practical and obviously knows the country from his own business experience."

Christian said tentatively, "How about you going out and seeing for yourself? Richard sent you an invitation anyway."

The result of that was that three days later Benedict arrived at Seeb Airport to be met by Belinda who made herself known to him, saying, "Richard sends his apologies but he had to fly down to Salala unexpectedly. He'll be back tonight."

He offered her a frankly admiring glance. "Christian said you'd changed," he told her smilingly, and she answered in an amused voice, "Yes, it's absurd isn't it — and I don't mean me. You and Christian — can anyone tell you apart?"

"I can't think of any offhand but it is possible."

On the way to the car, she said quite seriously, "You know, I've often wondered what it would feel like to be a twin; now I'll be able to find out, won't I? Are you alike inside as well as outside?"

He opened the car door for her before replying, quite familiar with this type of conversation. "As a matter of fact, we certainly are not. But that does not mean that we don't get on, if that is to be your next question."

She looked at him sharply before getting into the car. When they were both settled, she said contritely, "I'm sorry. That was a bad start. I didn't mean to be rude, but well — it was a bit of a shock to meet someone so like Christian. I hadn't thought about it before, and I hadn't remembered."

"Don't let it worry you, it's always happening. We are used to it. Now tell me where we are and where we are going," he asked as he stared round with interest.

She drove well and for the next hour gave him a comprehensive description of the country through which they were driving. Although he listened carefully, he mostly watched her as she drove. Christian's summing up had not done her justice, he thought, for, from where he sat, she was certainly extremely attractive judging from the profile he was studying. He was aware of high cheek-bones, short straight nose with a delicate jawline and a decidedly pointed chin which could lead to trouble. Eyes? Christian hadn't mentioned them and he had to get her to turn when he asked a question in order to find out what colour. Quite definitely green, he discovered, and her mouth was a trifle too wide and the freckles had changed to a light tan. Thick hair, still short, not red but a deep rich colour which caught the light as she moved.

She turned towards him again with a wide grin. "Yes, I *have* changed a bit haven't I?"

He realized that she had been aware of his scrutiny but decided not to apologize, only said, "Oh yes, quite a bit. Do you still play cricket? I seem to recollect that you were quite keen last time we met."

"You and Christian did nothing to encourage me so I gave it up and took up swimming instead. You know, I can't remember you and Christian being so alike then."

"We were, but you evidently didn't notice."

"I've brought a picnic lunch," she told him later, adding, "There's a lovely wadi soon and we'll have it there. It should be reasonably cool by the water."

When they arrived, he helped her out

with the picnic case, carrying it as near to the water as possible. Cool it was not after the air-conditioning of the car, but it was certainly a lovely spot. He asked her how she managed to look so cool and she said, "I'm not cool. Who could be in this, but I'm used to it and you have only just arrived. It comes as rather a shock after coming from an English winter."

"And, of course, I'll not be here long enough to become acclimatized."

"No, I suppose not. Particularly if you come to the conclusion that Christian was carried away and not being realistic."

"Is that what *you* think?" he asked quickly.

She answered slowly, "I did at first, but the more I thought about it the more attractive the idea became. It is certainly original. Anyway, wait until you see a dhow in the flesh, so to speak, before you decide against it."

"I'm keeping an open mind," he assured her. "Christian's ideas are usually pretty sound. That's why I am here." He walked down to the water's edge where it was fractionally cooler. They had driven through sandy desert but here, for the first time, he saw low green bushes on rocky ground near the water. In the distance there was the hazy outline of what looked like a castle, but Belinda told him that it was yet another fort. It was very quiet and peaceful and Benedict would have liked to linger but Belinda told him that they still had many miles to go and he helped her pack up the remains of a very good lunch and carry it back to the car.

They arrived at Sür in the early evening as Christian had done. There was no breeze and only the rim of the sun still showed on the edge of the horizon. Thankfully they subsided into the cool house with drinks while they sat quietly waiting for Richard to arrive.

2

THEY were finishing breakfast the following morning when Randal Kent arrived unheralded and coming into the room, looked at Benedict with surprise.

"My dear chap — I thought I was going to meet your brother. I'd no idea you were coming back."

Benedict took it in his stride, too used to this mistake to be thrown by it, but Belinda was amused and Richard hastened to put right the mistake. "This is Benedict, not Christian. I didn't realize that you did not know that they were twins."

Randal looked disconcerted but quickly recovered himself saying pleasantly, "No, I'd no idea. How interesting. You certainly are ridiculously alike. And — you are partners — how does that work out in business?"

He gave a slightly artificial laugh as he sat down and they were all aware that he was irritated at having made the mistake. In answer to his question Benedict said half seriously, "I don't think it has any effect at all." They talked then of the reason for his visit and Randal declared that he would be only too pleased to help in any way that he could.

Belinda offered him coffee and he picked up the English newspaper lying on a table. "Did you bring this with you?" he asked. "I see it is yesterday's date."

Benedict said, "No world-shaking news — only the usual depressing items, Irish bombs, rumours about the Royal family and the latest burglaries."

Randal smiled as he started to study the front page with interest. Belinda, watching him, wondered what had brought that rather mocking smile to his face. As if aware of her gaze, he said, "When I am out here I tend to lose track of what is going on in

England. There always seems plenty for the media to get their teeth into, true or false." He began to stir his coffee and changed the subject. "Obviously Christian told you about his scheme and that is why you are here."

From then on conversation was general and Belinda thought that Benedict was finding Randal impressive. Later, he took Benedict down to the shore where the men were working to introduce him to Hassan, the Omani ship-builder whom Christian had already met. From then on, it became clear that Christian's tentative idea was fast becoming a business proposition. Benedict embarked on drawing plans showing where changes would be necessary for the adaption for the tourist passengers. Difficulties were encountered and overcome with determination and, during this period, Randal Kent was fast becoming part of the general planning, pointing out that there must be space for the goods for import and export which he intended operating.

Belinda and Richard were almost as keen as Benedict himself and every evening closely examined the work he had been doing during the day on the plans.

"Randal seems to have muscled in on our scheme for his own business," Belinda said critically. "Do you really want that?"

Benedict, noticing her tone of voice, said mildly, "I can't see anything against it and he is anxious to invest in the idea too, and such a connection should be an asset."

She shrugged. "Yes, I suppose so."

"And," Benedict pointed out, "it's useful that he wants to put cash into the scheme."

She watched him complete a drawing. "Does it worry you, me standing watching you?"

He looked up with a quick smile. "On the contrary. I'm usually short of attractive girls standing by my side while I work. I'm enjoying the chance while it's there."

She felt the colour rise in her cheeks and was annoyed. He was only teasing and she was surprised at her own reaction. Surprised, too, that she was finding this man so attractive. She and Christian had got on well but she had felt no particular attraction, and now, here was his brother, a carbon copy who, without apparent effort, was making a very definite impression on her. What was it about this man which made him so different from his brother? Since they were identical, it could not be physical, so it had to be personality. She moved over to the window and he looked up.

"You really are interested, aren't you?"

"Yes, very much so. It really would be quite an achievement to make this a success. Dhows have played a large part in the history of this country and I think this idea is very exciting."

He pushed back his chair and went over to stand beside her. "You feel it too?" he asked. "Like something

15

coming alive again."

"Yes, that's it. Somehow they are more than just ships." Then she laughed. "We are waxing poetical aren't we? But just think of all the wonderful cargoes of spices, silks, dates, herbs and exotic fruits those ships have carried over hundreds of years. Frankincense and myrrh — such romantic cargoes." She paused, then, "And now we are proposing filling this ship with modern holidaymakers well roasted in the sun, all clamouring for bargains from the romantic ports they will visit."

He shrugged. "You sound cynical. The world goes on. This could be considered progress." He was only half serious, then added with a smile, "I can hardly complain since I am hoping to make money out of it. Come on — let's take a break."

They wandered down to the shore to walk on the sands. An old man sat crosslegged on the sand mending a huge net, further along some children were playing on a disintegrating wreck, their laughter sounding loud in the quiet air. Out in the bay small boats moved slowly on the smooth water, propelled from the stern by a single oar, seemingly without aim or purpose known to the watchers on the shore. It was relentlessly hot and in a few minutes, they made their way back to the house where fans were indolently stirring the air into some kind of coolness. In spite of the temperature Benedict found that it would not be difficult for this place to turn out to be addictive and, when after five days his plan had reached the stage when he needed to work with his brother in England, it was with great regret that he boarded a plane for Heathrow.

Belinda had driven him to Seeb and it was not until the last moment that he realized how much he was going to miss this girl who had proved such a pleasant companion. Looking into those expressive green eyes there had been a moment of indecision, then he leaned forward to kiss her gently on the lips before saying a final goodbye. Once on the plane, Benedict thought what a tepid parting it had been; how utterly unsatisfactory and not at all what he had intended until that moment of departure, and he simply didn't know how it had happened. With a grin, he wondered what Belinda had thought of it. He sat back. He would be returning, he thought comfortably. Now that Christian's dream was likely to come true there would be other opportunities and he decided that he would rectify the position as soon as he returned to Oman.

3

AT the airport Benedict spotted Christian before his brother saw him. He was standing staring straight in front of him looking grim. Benedict frowned, he knew that expression. It usually meant trouble of some kind; usually the sort which could have been avoided if more thought had been given to it. Of the two men, Christian was the more brilliant but the less stable, with a tendency to be carried away by the enthusiasm of the moment. It was for that reason that Benedict had been a trifle anxious about the present idea and had been relieved at the outcome, and now he was looking forward to discussing the latest news and plans with Christian and telling him that he approved of the whole scheme. He wondered what had gone wrong in the meantime. When Christian saw Benedict, he smiled broadly, his whole expression changing, his face showing sheer pleasure and Benedict was conscious of his usual glow at seeing him. There was a tremendous bond between them and although they were both so different in temperament, seldom had any serious disagreements.

As they met, Benedict decided not to ask any awkward questions. If Christian needed advice he would ask for it.

On the way down to Sussex with Christian driving, Benedict watched as he explained to him all he had been doing in Oman, and he was pleased to see him begin to relax. Perhaps he was mistaken in Christian's grim expression and it had only been due to anxiety about the present scheme and his own reaction to it and what he expected him to say. It was quite obvious that what Benedict was telling him gave him great satisfaction.

"You know, I was so certain that you'd turn it down and say it was one of my wild goose chases."

"Why were you so sure?"

Giving Benedict a quick glance, he said with a grin, "Well — you're a bit of a stick in the mud over new ideas and you don't always trust my judgement, but — " he hesitated, "but this time I had the backing of a man with a lot of experience and I hoped that might be a deciding factor."

Unexpectedly, Benedict asked, "You trust Randal Kent?"

Looking straight ahead Christian said, "Of course, why not?"

But Benedict wondered if there had been a slight hesitation before his brother had replied. He said, "He seems quite keen on his own account and is willing to invest some money in it if we make room for his exports and imports and that shouldn't be too difficult."

They talked on with Christian eager to see the plans Benedict had brought. Business was still slack and they would have time to work on them together.

With Richard and Randal acting as go-betweens, a genuine start was made on the project. It would be some weeks before much progress could be made and soon, one of them would have to return to Oman.

This time it had to be Christian and it was Randal who met him at the airport giving him a cheerful welcome which, oddly, Christian did not appear to appreciate. He sat quietly in the car as they started their long drive to Sür. The older man was giving a glowing report of the progress which had been made and, after a short while, Christian began asking questions and seemed satisfied with the answers Randal gave.

After a silence, he gave Christian a sidelong glance. "I hear that you were in London quite a lot. I am so glad you enjoyed the club. I thought you would and I am glad that you used it."

Christian said a trifle stiffly, "Yes, thank you for the introduction."

After a pause, Randal said, "I'm

sorry that it did not go better for you but I'm afraid that's the luck of the draw when you gamble."

Christian felt his colour rise. "How did you hear that?"

Randal looked surprised. "I told you — my cousin runs the club."

"So he keeps you posted on his clients' gambling losses?" Christian's tone was bitter.

"My dear chap, there is no need to take offence. Of course he doesn't keep me posted as you put it, but he knew that you came with my special introduction and he didn't want any unpleasantness."

Christian was silent for a few moments then he asked quietly, "Just what did he report to you?"

Randal took a hand from the wheel placing it for a second on Christian's knee.

"Don't let it worry you. We'll sort it out. It will be all right."

"What did he say?" Christian persisted.

Randal shrugged. "Only that there

had been an argument over your losses, that you disagreed with the amount."

"I still can't see how it could have been so much," Christian said stubbornly.

Randal laughed. "I'm afraid that is a common mistake to make. When you lose, it always seems more than you bargained for."

"Yes but — "

"Dear boy — I've already said don't let it worry you. I'll put matters right. I feel responsible as I introduced you and I'll send my cousin a cheque."

"No — I can't let you do that."

Randal said with an edge to his voice, "Then, what do you propose to do?"

There was a long silence which finally Randal broke, saying, "Now, don't worry, you and I can come to some agreement which will suit us both."

They were driving through the desert road and it was a long time before either of them spoke again, then Randal said meaningly, "I have the impression that your brother is not — well — enthusiastic about your gambling. Am I right?"

"As a matter of fact — yes."

"Then I imagine that he doesn't know of your — er — present predicament?"

"No. He doesn't."

"And you would prefer things to remain that way."

"Yes."

Another silence, then Randal said slowly, "I am not suggesting making you a present of the money. I told you, we can work out an arrangement which will suit us both, so stop worrying and just go along with it and — well — you don't really have any option, do you? Especially if you don't want your brother to know anything about it."

Christian supposed that the words should have been comforting, yet somehow they contained a menace he did not understand. Abruptly, the older man changed the subject saying, "Richard managed to get a short let on that apartment in which you were interested while the dhow is being built. I'm sure you will find it quite adequate for when either of you is over here."

Suddenly Christian found it very difficult to be grateful to this man who was taking so much trouble for Benedict and himself and for the remainder of the journey remained silent beside him, at this moment regretting the whole enterprise which had seemed so exciting at the beginning.

It was arranged that he should go direct to the apartment which had been rented for them and Randal stopped the car outside. Opening the door, Christian felt a sudden lift of the spirits. It looked clean and pleasant and he would be on his own, free to come and go as he pleased. Before leaving, Randal made it clear that they would be meeting the next day.

The rooms were adequate and comparatively cool and on the kitchen table was a note. "Supper in the fridge. See you in the morning. Belinda."

Instantly, Christian felt more cheerful. This, at least, was a pleasant welcome and he set off to find the promised meal, grateful for Belinda's thoughtfulness. In the car, he had felt too tired and dispirited to feel hungry but now when he saw the attractive salad and fish she had prepared, he enjoyed it though the thoughts which ran through his mind were not so pleasant. He had the uncomfortable feeling that in some way, Randal had set a trap for him, though in what way, he could not see. On the surface, the offer of help with his debt should have been a relief, but the manner in which it had been presented had been more in the nature of a warning. Christian sighed as he cleared the dishes he had used, suddenly feeling desperately tired after the long flight and the feeling of worry. Setting the dishes in the small sink, he decided to go to bed. Everything would appear better in the morning, he hoped forlornly. Perhaps he was imagining the threat in Randal's manner because of his own anxiety over the money he owed. Randal had hinted that in return for his paying off the debt Christian could be of some service to him. He was in no mood to try to work out what that service might be. It was not a vast sum and if they could help each other perhaps it could be settled amicably for both sides.

4

IN spite of the heat, Christian slept immediately, his next awareness, hearing sounds in the kitchen which he discovered was Belinda making toast and coffee. Surprised, he said, "I didn't expect to find you here making my breakfast. Will you join me?"

"No. I've had mine already, but I thought you might be pleased to find breakfast ready when you wakened." She poured coffee saying, "Richard had to leave early but he said would you join us for supper tonight? And Randal said would you meet him by the ship about eleven o'clock. All right?" she finished as she prepared to leave.

"Yes, and thanks for the invitation and for getting my breakfast. I'll meet Randal. Is he there often?"

Belinda smiled. "Yes, most days. He keeps a close watch on them. You'd

29

think it was his dhow."

Christian noticed that she sounded critical. He said, "Perhaps that's not a bad thing since neither Benedict nor I can be here all the time. After all, he has put some money into it."

"Yes, well, you can bet he'll have his money's worth. See you tonight," she added on her way out.

Six Omanis were working on the ship when Christian joined Randal at eleven o'clock and he was surprised at the amount of work which had been done. The three men talked together for some time but Christian was relieved when Randal left and he was able to deal with Hassan alone and he spent a further hour, at the end of which he felt he had gained more useful knowledge. If it had not been for the nagging worry in his mind, he would have been feeling very happy at the way their new venture was shaping.

At dinner that night, they all enjoyed exchanging news and Richard was pleased that Christian was satisfied with the progress which had been made.

"I'm delighted. I didn't expect to find it so advanced. It's most exciting."

Watching him, Belinda wondered what it was about Benedict which affected her so differently from this man who was his double; the same dark-blue eyes, dark-brown hair, similar features, yet, to her, completely different. She couldn't explain it, but it was a fact.

Later, the phone rang, Belinda took it and handed it to Christian.

"Randal here. Will you join me for lunch tomorrow? Just a working lunch at my house."

Christian agreed with some reluctance and, when he told them, Richard said mildly, "Well, he tries to be helpful," and Christian agreed quickly.

The next day, he walked the short distance to Randal's house and was taken by an Omani girl through a cool tiled hall to a shaded terrace behind the house.

Randal, looking cool in an open-necked shirt, came forward to meet him and his appearance made Christian feel even hotter than he was already. Indicating a chair, Randal offered iced drinks. Anywhere else, Christian would have felt relaxed on this terrace with the exotic flowers, instead, he was tense; but Randal kept the conversation light until the Omani girl came to announce lunch.

It was not until they returned to the terrace after the meal and Randal was pouring coffee that he said almost casually, "Well now, let's get this little matter settled, shall we?" He handed Christian a cup. "How much do you owe?"

Christian said quietly, "I am not happy at all about this."

Randal shrugged. "No, I don't suppose you are but what other suggestion have you for paying your debt?" Suddenly it was another man speaking, his voice cold as he picked up a pen and drew a cheque book towards him.

His voice tentative, Christian said, "I

think you mentioned some arrangement which would be of benefit to us both?"

"Yes. That's fair, isn't it?"

"Of course — only — "

Randal raised his eyebrows. "Only — what?"

"Only I must know what my commitment is before accepting your offer."

Randal picked up his cup taking a careful sip before replying.

"You are aware that my business consists largely of imports and exports." He put down the cup. "You also know that I now have a small share in the ship in order that I can use a space for my business."

"Yes, I am aware of that, but I imagine that what you are suggesting is something beyond that?"

With a cold smile, Randal agreed, pouring more coffee into his cup before saying, "It is sometimes convenient for me to ship a few additions to orders, well — more privately, you understand?"

He waited, and Christian said with brutal frankness, "I think you mean shipping something illegally." It was a statement and his tone was contemptuous.

Randal shrugged. "The — rules — sometimes make things unnecessarily difficult for a customer."

Christian received this new angle silently, finally saying, "You are, I think, suggesting that I break the law."

Randal smiled coldly. "Your only duty would be to see that the package in question was delivered safely. For that simple operation, I am prepared to clear your debt."

Christian said clearly, "A sort of blackmail."

Randal laughed. "An unpleasant word and entirely unnecessary in this instance. I promised mutual assistance. It is as simple as that. But, of course, you have a choice."

"Choice?" The one word held contempt.

"Certainly. You can refuse my offer and decide to face the consequences of your foolishness, but I should warn you, my cousin is difficult to deal with and he would be certain to bring a case against you which would not enhance your firm at a time which is proving difficult anyway." He paused. "And it would trouble you to forfeit your brother's good opinion I think." He stood up. "You don't have to decide today. Let me know tomorrow."

As they reached the front door, Randal said quietly, "I think it would not be wise to mention this conversation to your friends."

Without turning, Christian went through the door which Randal was holding open.

He was scarcely aware of the heat as he walked back to the flat, angry as much with himself as with Randal. It had been Randal who had introduced him to his cousin's gambling club in London, but his own love of the game which had ended in disaster. Because Benedict had never approved of his gambling, he had not mentioned his visits to the club. He looked at his watch as he went inside and sat down. He was due to meet Hassan at the site.

For a few minutes, he remained slumped in his chair. He had until tomorrow to come to a decision. But already he knew what that decision would be: there was no real choice.

5

CHRISTIAN slept badly again, partly due to the heat, but mostly because of an unquiet mind. As soon as it was light he rose and, drawn as he always was by the fascination of the ship, he walked down to the shore. The men were already at work in the comparative cool of the early morning.

Two small children were playing on a huge stack of loosely packed timbers, the boy clambering higher each second, laughing down at the little girl who was shrieking at him to come down. His answer to her pleas was to climb higher and in doing so, dislodged a heavy beam which started the rest moving. With a terrified scream, he disappeared in the shambles of shifting timbers and Christian started running towards it. When he reached the spot, there was no sign of the child at ground level but, looking up, he caught a glimpse of a small body which seemed to be wedged in a tangle of wood.

Testing each foothold, Christian struggled to reach him, knowing that each step might cause a further avalanche. Finally, directly above the child he searched for a way of reaching down to free him, then he heard it, the soft menacing sound of shifting wood, sliding from above him, first in slow motion, then with increasing speed and he knew that he could do nothing to stop it except to fling himself forward in a vain attempt to shield the boy as it finally crashed down. It all happened too fast for clear thought; the final impact beyond anything he could have imagined, followed almost immediately by blessed oblivion.

His next conscious thought was seeing Hassan's face bending over him as he lay on the sands. He knew the question he needed to ask but could not form the words, but as if he understood

Hassan said, with tears streaming down his face, "My son — he lives — you saved him."

It should have been a moment of triumph for Christian but his own agony filled his mind. He tried to move and blacked out again and his next memory was of being carefully lifted into an ambulance and given an injection.

A long time later, he realized that he was in hospital and became conscious that someone sat beside him. As soon as he opened his eyes, it was Randal Kent who said, "I hear you have been playing the hero. A splendid effort — you have made a friend for life with Hassan. He adores that boy and you have earned his eternal gratitude."

It was a long speech in the voice which Christian least wanted to hear. Somehow, it grated on his nerves, but he managed to ask about the boy.

"In the same hospital, and he is going to be all right. You certainly saved his life."

Randal stood up, looking down at Christian as he lay in the bed. "This will slow us down a bit, but everything remains the same. I wanted you to know." After a pause, he asked, "Had you come to a decision?"

Christian was not feeling in the mood for decisions but sudden anger overtook him. He struggled to sit up, found he could not move except to turn his head towards Randal. "If this is anything to do with drugs, whatever the consequences, I will not touch it."

It was with surprise that he saw an expression of genuine horror on Randal's face.

"Drugs? I wouldn't touch them under any circumstances," he said indignantly, and such was the tone of his voice that Christian had no difficulty in believing him. Having shot that bolt, he turned his head away leaving the next move to Randal and there was a short silence before he said quietly, "I told you that your only duty would be to hand over the goods to someone who will collect them."

"And where will this collection take place? I imagine not in England since you intend using the ship for your own business."

"You imagine correctly. I understand that you are planning to join the first trip in any case, and your sole task would be to hand over the goods to the person who comes to claim them. Quite simple." He stood looking down at Christian with a contemptuous expression as he said coldly, "Hardly an onerous undertaking with no risk to yourself and one which has the advantage of leaving you free of debt."

With great difficulty, Christian turned his head to face him. "How do I know that I can trust you?"

Randal gave a short laugh. "Don't be childish. We have to trust each other since we are both profiting from the enterprise. The whole success rests on mutual trust. That is an essential for both of us." He was talking as if the terms were finally agreed.

Christian asked sharply, "And the cheque? When do I get that?"

Randal, seeing that he had won, allowed himself a smile. "At the same time that you take delivery of the goods. That's fair enough, isn't it?"

Christian didn't answer and, after a moment, Randal pointed out that there was no immediate hurry as they had to wait until the ship was completed.

Christian frowned, "What about your cousin — will he wait?" He too, was now speaking as if the decision had already been made.

With a wave of his hand, Randal dismissed any difficulty. "If I tell him that the debt will be paid, he will wait."

Christian suddenly felt desperately tired. There was no point in arguing. He had no real alternative. He might as well agree now. He was not happy about any of it and he was still suspicious of this man's business methods but with the weight of that debt hanging over him, the thought of being free of it was worth the niggling anxiety of the method being applied to bring that about. He had to trust Randal. He had to accept that his only responsibility would be to deliver the goods.

"So," Randal said affably. "We settle a gentleman's agreement and wait for the famous first voyage to commence. I feel certain that when the time comes, the tour will be fully booked." He turned towards the door. "Well, I'll leave you now, you must feel like resting. I am glad that we have been able to arrive at such an amicable arrangement. Your accident was most unfortunate and I hope that you make a quick recovery. The boy was certainly lucky that you were there. Hassan is entirely right to be so grateful and I feel sure he will do everything he can for you in the future."

It was all said in a friendly manner but Christian noticed the stressing of Hassan's gratitude and wondered if perhaps in some way Randal resented that Hassan should now feel that he owed a debt to Christian. At the moment, his head throbbed and every part of him pained him. He closed his eyes and tried not to think of anything but didn't meet with any great success.

6

WHEN Hassan visited Christian later, he was effusive in his gratitude for the safety of his son. "I watched," he said. "From below I watched and I could do nothing. I saw that you stopped the beam from killing him. It was so brave what you did. I am grateful." He paused, his dark eyes swimming as he searched for the right words to express his feelings. "I will do all I can for you. You will trust me — yes? I will try to see that — " He hesitated, then continued slowly, "I will try to see that everything is right for you. It is my duty now." Again he paused, looking anxiously at Christian, then finished on a question. "You understand?"

Bewildered by the oddness of his manner Christian realized that the man was worried and that his anxiety was not connected with his son's accident, but with Randal and his own job. If Randal was involving Hassan in any of his schemes, then Christian had no doubt that it was likely to be outside the law. An assumption not difficult to arrive at after his own experience of the man with whom he was being forced to do business through his own stupidity. Once clear of this, he vowed that he would never gamble again. Far from satisfied at the way things had gone, he was, nevertheless, thankful that there was no connection with drugs.

But now, there seemed problems with Hassan. How much did the man know of Randal's business? How deeply was he involved? What he had said had surely been in the nature of a warning. Had Hassan's loyalties changed because Christian had saved his son's life? Christian stared into those troubled dark eyes and asked a question of his own.

"What should I understand?"

Hassan looked away, shrugging his

shoulders and it was a moment before he said slowly, "There are — changes."

"Changes? What kind of changes?"

"In the construction. Only small but — changes."

"You mean — different from my original plan?"

"Yes. Different."

"And this was Mr Kent's idea?"

Suddenly light dawned and Christian said, "You mean a special place built into the ship? Like a hiding place?"

"Yes — that is it."

"And Mr Kent didn't want you to tell me?" That was really a statement, not a question. Relief spread over Hassan's face as he nodded.

"Mr Kent paid you money for this?"

"Yes, he said it was only a practical change which would be useful, but that you might not like your plan changed so — better not to say."

"And you believed that this change was entirely innocent?"

Christian's voice held a note of angry contempt and Hassan would not meet his eyes as he said, "I did not know of any other reason. I thought it — perhaps odd but — " He hesitated then added weakly, "You see — it was not my business — so — better not to ask."

"Especially as you were being paid to keep quiet," Christian said angrily, very aware of the pounding pain in his head and of the fact that it was becoming clearer every minute that there were hidden angles here with himself caught in the trap through his own foolishness.

Hassan spread his hands in a helpless gesture. "Mr Kent explained that this private space might be for the valuables of the passengers — you understand?"

"But, you didn't believe him, did you?"

"It seemed odd," he said, shaking his head, standing awkwardly at the end of Christian's bed. Finally Christian came to a decision. He couldn't think clearly because of the pain in his head and he needed time to think.

Speaking slowly, he said, "You must not mention to anyone what you have just told me. You must carry on exactly the same way. I need time to think about this. It is very important."

Hassan looked frightened as he said, "I knew I had to tell you." He paused, adding, "Because you saved my son's life."

It was a naive statement which made it clear that if the accident had not happened, Hassan would have remained silent. Christian closed his eyes wearily. "I am glad that you have told me, but it is important that I think what must be done. I will see you again and, in the meantime, keep your own counsel and continue to do what Mr Kent tells you."

Inclining his head in a small bow Hassan turned and walked out of the room and Christian lay back with a small sigh. He felt battered and bruised all over and completely exhausted. Suddenly he longed for Benedict, torn between his wish that his brother should not know of his stupid weakness through his love of gambling and his desperate need to discuss and assess this worrying situation which had arisen. Throughout their lives they had shared both trouble and success, but it was always Benedict who had led with his clear sight and determination. Only now did Christian fully realize how much he depended on his brother. At the moment, he felt completely useless. The doctors were not prepared to let him leave hospital for several days and, even when he did, he would not be very mobile for some time and so would be very much at Randal's mercy, for now he was convinced that the man was dangerous and engaged in something far more serious than Christian had at first supposed. Something which, at the moment, he could do nothing to prevent. The only small advantage he could think of was that now he was in possession of important knowledge which Randal didn't know he had; but he still needed to know a great deal more than Hassan could tell him. His own position was extremely precarious and he had to find out Randal's real business.

In spite of his pain, he must have slept and he wakened to the sound of the door opening. The light was fading and it took him a few seconds to recognize the figure crossing the room to his bed. When he did, he was not prepared for the sudden flood of relief which poured through him.

"Benedict — I'd no idea that you were coming, or that you even knew what had happened. Who told you?"

Benedict stood for a moment, looking down at his brother. "What a mess. Did you have to go in for heroics on such a grand scale?"

The words sounded unsympathetic but his eyes were full of anxiety as he added, "Belinda rang me."

Christian said, "It's good to see you, but how did you manage to leave?"

"There's not much doing at the moment. Mansell will be able to cope."

51

Christian said slowly, "I'm sorry to be such a damned nuisance."

"Hassan told Belinda that you saved the boy's life and took the weight of the fall yourself."

Conscious of the pride in his brother's voice, Christian smiled. "You'd hardly expect me to duck, would you?"

And Benedict said crisply, "No, as a matter of fact, I wouldn't." Changing the subject abruptly, he continued, "As soon as you are out of here you'd better come home. You won't be mobile for some time and things are going well here."

Christian frowned, saying, "One of us will have to be here."

Benedict glanced sharply at him aware of the anxiety in his voice.

"What's wrong?"

"I don't know yet."

"But, there *is* something?"

"I'm afraid so, yes."

And with these words, Christian knew that he had decided to tell Benedict the whole story.

7

THEY talked for an hour, with Christian making no excuses for his own part in what had happened. "But," he said, "I still can't understand that the amount could have been so large. I've been through bad patches at other times, but I've never gambled more than I could afford, and I thought — " He stopped abruptly as he saw Benedict's expression.

"Didn't it occur to you that you might be being set up?"

Christian shook his head. "No. Not at that time. Why should it? What reason could there be?"

Benedict said grimly, "That is what we are going to find out because from all you have been telling me this is not as straightforward as you supposed. I am convinced that Randal is using you for some purpose of his own."

He paused, moving restlessly round the small room. "You seem certain that it is not drugs so we have to think again and obviously some kind of theft comes to mind, but I fail to see what use you could be to him."

Christian said wearily, "He simply said that if I agreed to deliver something for him he would clear my debt."

"And this was to take place during the first voyage?"

"Yes. He knew that I intended to be on that trip."

Benedict stopped his pacing to stand looking down at his brother. "If only you had told me."

"You've always been against my gambling and I didn't want to worry you. I've always managed before, only small amounts. In any case, what could you have done?"

"That's obvious. I could have paid the money and none of this would have happened."

After a moment, Christian said slowly, "Perhaps that is just what

Randal didn't want. If this *is* a set up, this way he's got me just where he wanted me. But for what reason I have no idea."

Benedict looked at his watch. "Belinda's picking me up here, I must go. Try not to worry. We still have some time before any of this happens and I am determined to discover what Randal's game is."

Looking exhausted, Christian said, "I'm sorry Benedict. It won't happen again. I've really learned my lesson this time."

For the first time, Benedict said impatiently, "But you're not out of the wood yet."

"No. I know that, but as soon as I can move I intend to get to the bottom of this if it's the last thing I do."

Benedict's expression suddenly softened and he smiled at the heavily bandaged figure in the bed. "Well, you may have been a bloody fool over your gambling but you certainly did a good job for the boy and Hassan couldn't be more grateful." He turned to the door saying, "As soon as you are ready, we will fly home."

The door opened just as he reached it and Belinda came in carrying magazines and fruit. Christian watched as Benedict and Belinda met. It was, he thought, like a collision of eyes and he was conscious of a sense of shock. He had known that Benedict was attracted but this was more than that; this was love and, absurdly, he suddenly wondered if his brother realized it himself.

The next minute they were exchanging normal greetings and Belinda came over to the bed saying lightly to Benedict, "What do you think of our local hero?"

They talked for a few minutes, then Belinda and Benedict left together.

She asked, "What do you think of him?"

"He's pretty bashed up, but he is worried as well."

Frowning as she got into the car,

she asked, "Worried? But the boy is all right, isn't he?"

"Yes — it's not the boy. It's Randal Kent."

"Why — what has he done?" She asked the question then added quickly, "No, don't tell me now. Richard is home and I'm taking you back for supper. Is that all right for you? Tell us both then; Richard will want to hear as well. You know, what Christian did was wonderful. He saved the child's life and he might have been killed himself. Hassan is terribly grateful."

At home Richard was waiting for them and over drinks, Benedict told them the story Christian had confided in him. As the details became clear Richard looked more and more surprised. "I can't believe it. What's the man playing at? Surely he would not interfere with the design of the ship unless it is something on a big scale. You say that Christian believed him when he said it was not drugs?"

"Yes. He seems certain of that."

Benedict moved impatiently. "I can't understand why Christian didn't tell me at once."

Belinda said quietly, "Because he values your good opinion. He didn't want you to know how foolish he had been."

"But he knew I would have helped him."

Richard said, "He doesn't seem to know how much he lost."

"The whole thing is crazy," Benedict said angrily. "Randal and his cousin must be in this together and got Christian where they can manipulate him into accepting Randal's help so that they can use him."

"It would help if we had some idea of what they are up to," Belinda said sharply.

"It seems that Christian is to be used as some sort of delivery boy and that is all." Richard sounded disbelieving and Benedict nodded. "The whole thing sounds like some silly game, but I think it is far from that if he has bribed Hassan to build in a secret space on the ship."

"And don't forget," Belinda said impatiently, "that he is banking on Christian not telling Benedict anything at all, so, what's the wretched man up to if it isn't drugs?"

"Obviously something valuable and presumably not too large — and — surely it has to be stolen."

Richard said quickly, "We don't *know* that."

Belinda suggested with some irritation, "You are still reluctant to believe anything against him. Can't you see that his import/export business would be an ideal way of disposing of stolen goods?"

"It would have to be very carefully done."

"Well, isn't that exactly what he is planning to do? Isn't that why he is proposing to use Christian as his delivery boy, so that if anything goes wrong Christian will be the person to take the blame while Randal comes out of it innocent, having been taken in by a friend he trusted?"

Benedict looked at her with a broad grin. "You're really serious, aren't you? But so far, there isn't a shadow of anything against this man. In fact, the only thing he has done so far is to help Christian pay off a large debt."

"In return for Christian delivering an unknown package," Belinda scoffed. "That sounds a bit weak — and that was before the accident which seems to have changed everything, for now, through Hassan, we know about the secrecy which has been going on." She stopped, frowning. "If it hadn't been for the accident and Hassan being grateful to Christian, we shouldn't have known anything about it, or that anything was wrong."

Benedict was watching her closely and she heard him sigh deeply.

"Yes, I know all that, but we still have some time to sort it all out. It won't be easy, but I certainly intend to try." He crossed the room to her, holding out his hand. "Come with me and have a look at the ship in the moonlight."

Richard allowed himself a small smile as they drifted out of the room and made for the shore.

8

THE weather in England was providing an almost perfect spring and Christian was improving daily although his back was still painful when he walked far. Both brothers were pleased that new orders were coming in with the better weather and they were both busy. They kept in constant touch with Oman and news of the building of the dhow. Kent had kept his word and kept them up to date with progress. Richard too, seemed satisfied with what was taking place. Since they now knew that Randal had such a close interest in the project, they had no doubts that work would be kept up to date.

Through a business friend, Benedict had been trying to find out more about Randal's London office and business methods, so far with little success.

Benedict tossed a letter across the breakfast table to Christian saying, "Patrick seems to think that we are wasting both his and our time. Read that."

"I have made all the enquiries you asked for with absolutely no result except that your friend seems specially anxious to make plain to all concerned that he is as honest as the day in all his dealings. Almost too anxious, perhaps? Too much stress on honesty? In other words, the lily is, perhaps almost too pure for belief!"

"I wonder what that last part means?" Christian wondered as he handed back the letter.

"Evidently Patrick feels that Randal proclaims his honesty too strongly. Anyhow, that won't help us."

Christian said slowly, "No, but I'm not convinced of his honesty, but there doesn't seem anything more that we can do now."

They were interrupted by the phone and Benedict went to answer it, coming

63

back into the room a few minutes later, his face wreathed in smiles. "Belinda's in England. She's coming down."

Christian looked at his brother solemnly. "The idea doesn't seem to depress you unduly," he observed drily. "When is she coming?"

"Tomorrow. She sounded most mysterious."

"About what?"

Benedict shook his head. "No idea, she wouldn't say. She is coming by train and I am meeting her. I thought she could have the room overlooking the quay."

Benedict's mood had changed and Christian smiled widely. "You decided all that very quickly," he pointed out as he began to clear the breakfast china.

Benedict returned his smile, saying, "Well, aren't *you* pleased that she is coming?"

Carrying the tray, Christian spoke over his shoulder. "Oh yes, but not demented as you seem to be." Continuing to the kitchen, he let the door close behind him, and was still laughing as he saw that Biddy had arrived.

Biddy they had known all their lives and she often treated them as if they were still children and said now as she tied an apron round her middle, "I suppose you've not had the sense to rest as the doctor told you, and you shouldn't be carrying that tray either."

He put the tray on the table assuring her that it was necessary for him to exercise his back muscles, suddenly very aware that the tray had not been the best way of doing it. "We're having a visitor tomorrow," he told her now. "One you know," he added quickly. Biddy was not exactly enthusiastic about casual visitors.

"And who is it coming to disturb our peace?" she wanted to know.

"You remember Belinda? The redhead?"

Biddy's expression changed. "Oh — her. I don't call her a visitor. Nothing but a tomboy. Always trying

65

to beat you boys at whatever you were doing."

"She's changed a bit Biddy. Not so much of the tomboy — more of an attractive young lady now."

She peered at him suspiciously. "Coming to see *you*, is she? Or is it your brother she's after?"

"I don't think there is any question of her being after either of us as a matter of fact. More that Benedict is after her in a big way, I'd say."

Biddy bridled. "And what about you? Don't *you* fancy her? You've got as good a chance, I'm sure. I don't suppose she can tell you apart anyway. So, what's going to happen about *that*, I'd like to know?"

He said solemnly, "Well, that'll make it all very exciting, won't it?"

She gave him a frowning glance. "You wouldn't do that to the poor girl, would you?" For answer, he asked, "Which of us are you talking to now?"

"Christian," she answered promptly and he laughed.

"If you can do it, so can she. She has known us as long as you have. No doubt she has got us taped."

Having settled that problem he went out and across the yard to the office where he worked and she noticed that he was still using his stick.

The next morning, he was not surprised when Benedict allowed far too much time to meet Belinda but refrained from commenting on the fact. It was becoming obvious that this time, his brother was severely smitten. When he finally heard the car turn into the yard, he went out to meet them, himself delighted to see Belinda again looking remarkably attractive in a plain cream suit which seemed to set alight her red hair. They stood chatting for a few minutes before Benedict became impatient.

"Come on. Let's go in. She's refusing to unravel the mystery until we are all together and I can't wait to hear what it is."

Walking through the hall Belinda

sniffed the air. "Lovely smell of wood. You've got a fire, how nice," and she gave a contented sigh as she crossed the room to the huge open fireplace with its burning logs. "I love being in Oman, but it's lovely to come home. It's not really cold today, but this is such a lovely fire, and this time of year is just right, with everything in bud and new." Both men looked at her with broad grins.

"You're spinning it out, aren't you? Now, come on, don't make us wait any longer to hear your news. What has happened?"

9

FOR answer, she went over to a table where she had laid down her bag. Under it was a carefully folded newspaper which she now spread out on the table. Standing back with a triumphant air, she said, "There — what do you think of that?"

She was pointing to a small photograph halfway down the page. Above it headlines announced that there had been another big burglary which had resulted in the loss of valuable paintings, silver and clocks. The police were working on the theory that the present raid was done by the same expert team who carried out a similar burglary some months ago only a few miles away. The photograph reproduced on the page, and now published for the first time, was a small painting by the elder

Wainwright which was stolen in the previous raid and it was hoped that this reproduction might jog someone's memory who could possibly have seen the painting somewhere recently. If so, the article asked that they please get in touch with the police immediately.

The two men studied the newspaper with puzzled interest before Christian said, "Why all the interest? *We've* not seen it."

Belinda moved impatiently. "No, but *I* have."

After an astonished silence, Benedict asked quietly, "Where? When did you see it?"

"I'm almost certain, and I can check." Her voice held excitement and Benedict asked again impatiently, "How could you have seen it? Where?"

She answered slowly, each word stressed. "Hanging in Randal's sitting-room."

Both men stared, trying to take in what she had just said. Finally Christian asked, "What exactly are you saying?"

"Don't you see? Don't you understand? If I am right, there must be a connection between Kent and these burglaries." The silence lasted a long time before he said slowly, "But how? I mean — surely that is unlikely?"

She said quickly, "It may be unlikely, but think about it — think about what he is doing on the ship — and what he is making you do. Can't you see what an outlet this could be for him, an opportunity to pass on stolen goods to other countries without any apparent connection with himself?"

"You are suggesting that he is planning to hide stuff on the ship — then pass it on at various ports." Benedict spoke slowly then turned to Christian. "What would be the point of you being involved?"

Christian shook his head. "All I know is that I am to deliver — packets which would be picked up at various ports." He paused. "Doesn't seem to make much sense, does it?"

Belinda walked over to the fire,

stretching out her hands to the blaze. "Is that all you are supposed to do?"

"That's what he said, but well — any of the crew could do that."

Belinda stood staring into the fire, her spread fingers seeming almost transparent in the glow of the logs. Suddenly, she turned to face them.

"No. None of the crew would know what went into that extra space that had been built and that is where your package would have been and you would be the only person who knew about it."

Her words fell into a silence while both men considered what she had said. At last, Benedict said, "I can't help feeling that we are assuming a lot. I mean, we don't really *know* any of this."

"No, but it slots very neatly into place doesn't it?"

He frowned. "Yes, that's rather what I am afraid of. It's *too* neat. It would be too much of a risk for Randal. We are not dealing with things of small value but worth thousands of pounds."

"Which would most certainly be a lot safer disposed of in this way than nearer home, or anywhere else, for that matter."

They were all silent, busy with their own thoughts. Benedict began pacing the room watched by the others. Finally he said, regretfully, "No, I'm afraid there is too much wishful thinking about this. You know what Patrick said in his letter — there is not a whisper against him in his business. He would have too much to lose if this went wrong." He turned to Belinda. "What would you like — an early drink or a cup of tea?"

She chose tea and he went out to the kitchen and they heard him setting a tray with a clatter. In the sitting-room Belinda said, "I know I could be wrong, but when I saw that photograph I was so convinced that I'd seen it before. At first, I couldn't think where, then I remembered one day when I went to Randal's villa to pick up some papers he had brought back from England for Richard. The maid left me in the sitting-room while she went to fetch Randal." She paused, her eyes narrowed, seeing again that day. "The more I think of it the more certain I am."

Coming into the room carrying a tray, Benedict said, "Even if you are right it probably wouldn't be there now."

The brightness left her face as she looked at him. "I hadn't thought of that. You mean, he wouldn't dare to keep it?"

Before Benedict could reply Christian said, "What risk would there be? Thousands of miles away and at that time absolutely no reason for him to be connected with it. He could have bought the painting quite innocently."

Benedict put down the tray and began pouring tea, then handed a cup to Belinda. He said, "Yes, I suppose that it would have been safe enough then, but now, it no longer will be."

Pointing to the newspaper Belinda said quickly, "You mean because of this?"

"Yes, it might not be so easy if someone saw it on the wall and made the connection."

"It would be a long chance for that to happen," Christian said.

Belinda laughed. "It's a long chance which I hope is going to happen," she announced with some glee. "I'm taking back some office papers from England for him and I shall be delivering them to him as soon as I arrive back in Oman. At least that will give me a chance to look and see if it is still there."

"Do you do this postman act often?" Christian enquired.

"Yes, lots of firms do it. It saves time and we help each other. It's more or less an accepted thing."

"When do you have to return?"

"The late flight Friday. Randal's office will deliver what papers there are to our London office and I will pick them up before I leave." She laughed. "I think you can guarantee that whatever I'm carrying will be entirely innocent."

Benedict said, "I don't want you taking any risks when you go to Randal's house."

"What risks could I be taking? I am only delivering stuff he has been waiting for."

"Well if you don't see the painting where you saw it before, don't go searching for it elsewhere."

"Don't worry. In any case, it is quite likely that it has been out of the house for weeks." She stopped, then added, "I'm not so sure though. Randall has a genuine love of art. He might take a risk and keep it."

"Not if he's seen this copy of the newspaper," Christian suggested.

"That's a point; but we shan't know until I walk innocently into his house with the papers I've so kindly brought for him."

They talked for some time before

Benedict, taking her arm, suggested showing her her room and, as soon as they reached it, he put his arms round her, holding her close. "I've been waiting for that," he told her some minutes later. "I wish you didn't have to go back. Do you ever feel lonely?"

She shook her head. "No, not really. Richard and I both work and I come home on leave fairly frequently."

"You like the life?"

"Yes. Life is never dull."

"Men?" he asked.

"Yes, men," she agreed with a smile.

"One?"

She hesitated. "In a way, yes. More of a friend."

"How much does he mean to you?"

She was very conscious of him standing close to her. "I have known him ever since I went out to Oman."

"So — you know him well?"

"Yes, of course I know him well."

He hesitated. "And — what does that mean?"

She laughed. "Not what you appear to think it does."

He joined her at the window, standing beside her without touching her.

"How serious?"

"I think Richard would be quite pleased if I married him."

"I see."

"No. You don't. I don't need my brother to choose my husband."

"But, you are fond of him."

"Of course. He is an old friend."

"So?"

"So it means that I make up my own mind who I want to spend the rest of my life with." She paused, finally saying, "For me, marriage would have to be for life so — I have to be very sure."

His hands came up to hold her face as he looked into her eyes saying, "For myself I am very sure, but if I have any chance at all — take all the time you want to decide if you want to live your life with me. I can only tell you that I love you very much and that I know that will not change." Kissing her very gently on the lips, he let her go saying, "I will try to be patient and not to assume too much."

After he left her, Belinda continued to stand by the open window, her thoughts scattered between two countries, between two men. A cold breeze suddenly blew into the room and she shivered, turning to close the window. Did she really need to hesitate? Did she really need to think? When had she ever considered Slade in the context of a husband? It had been an easy relationship over the years she had been there. One which, she thought, suited them both. Had it ever been more than that? Probably not, but had Benedict not appeared, it was one which might have drifted into something more serious. They had many of the same interests, met at many of the same places. It had been pleasant, but not intense on either side, she thought. Slade was a tall, handsome man, kind and generous, fun to be with. The sort of man any girl might be delighted to marry and, she was very fond of him. And Benedict? What did she feel for him? What she felt for Benedict was something totally different. Something — . She searched for the right word and the one she came up with was, *uncomfortable*. She smiled. What an extraordinary word to think of. What did she mean by it? Because she was constantly aware of him; because she felt, and required his strength; because she loved the sound of his voice, the touch of his hands, his nearness. Because she felt incomplete without him. She moved impatiently. What a list. What did it prove? Surely she was setting out quite clearly, the state of being in love.

It was nearly dark now, quite dark in the room, but outside lights were reflected in the water; there were lighted windows and, above, the moon was lightly covered by cloud. She turned to the door, opened it and went down the wide stairs to join the men below.

Belinda left Sussex the following morning, her stay having been far too short but back at Sür, there was much to discuss, with Belinda telling Richard about the English burglaries, showing him the newspaper shot and explaining her plan.

"And if he has already removed the painting?"

"Well, that in itself would look odd."

Richard shook his head. "Randal has a pretty good name here, especially with the authorities. He *could* have bought that painting quite innocently."

"But, if he sees that shot in the paper he will certainly be worried." Belinda paused, then ended crisply, "So, the sooner I get there the better."

10

THE next morning, Belinda drove to Randal Kent's house carrying the case which held the papers she had brought for him. She stood for a moment before knocking at the lovely carved front door. She was surprised to find that her heart was beating rather too fast. She and Richard had been dinner guests several times in this house but this was the first time she had come to bring any papers she had brought back for him as he usually fetched them himself. Suddenly she felt that she was in the wrong place for the wrong reason. She must remember to behave casually.

The Omani girl who opened the door to her showed her into the room where she had seen the painting and, as soon as she was alone, she walked slowly round the room. There were no large pictures on the walls but many small and medium-sized ones and she was conscious of a small thrill when she came to a space. She was standing in front of it when she heard his voice behind her.

"You are interested in art?"

Startled, she turned quickly to see Randal Kent standing in the doorway. In his hand, he held a small painting. His eyes were narrowed as he looked at her and she imagined that she saw suspicion in them. It was unfortunate that she had paused at the empty space just as he came into the room. She recovered herself quickly, saying ruefully, "I'm afraid I know nothing about art, only that I love looking at lovely pictures." She finished with an appreciative wave of her hand. "And you have plenty of those." She wondered as she spoke how many of those on the wall in front of her had been stolen.

Coming further into the room, he set down the picture he was carrying against the wall saying, "I change them round from time to time. It is nice to have a change — makes you more aware of them. In any case, the light didn't seem right for the one which was hanging there and I am hoping that this one will be more suitable." He bent to pick it up, holding it to the wall. "What do you think?"

She stood back to look at it then, greatly daring, said, "Yes. The light seems right for this one. Was the subject of the other one very different?"

Her voice was innocent but she was conscious of his sharp glance and his hesitation before he answered. "Yes. It was a rather colourful desert scene." He hesitated, "You don't remember it?"

She shook her head. "Afraid not, but as I said, I am not up in art, but this painting looks lovely and seems to fit very well."

He moved away from the wall, turning to give her one of his appreciative stares which she never cared for then, smiling, he said, "To what do I owe this unexpected visit?"

Belinda pointed to the table where she had left the case. "Why, I've brought the papers you were expecting from England."

For a second, he frowned saying, "But I always call in for them. You shouldn't have bothered to bring them."

She said lightly, "No bother at all. I had to come in to the Suq and it seemed silly not to bring the case with me."

Once again, she was conscious of slight tension in him as he thanked her, adding, "There will be coffee waiting for us. Please come."

Feeling that there was no option, she followed him out to the patio at the back of the house which always seemed to be cool. Pouring coffee, he asked her for news of Christian.

"His shoulder is still painful and he still limps, but he is certainly better," Belinda told him.

"I know that it is his wish to go on the first trip, do you think he will be fully recovered by then?"

She didn't for a moment doubt his personal interest in Christian's health since it was on this voyage that he was to undertake his delivery jobs which were to clear his debt to Randal. She said now cheerfully, "Oh yes, I think so. There is still quite a lot of time and I'm sure he hopes to be out again before that."

They talked then of the dhow and its future and all the time, sitting opposite him, she was unpleasantly aware that he watched her with the expression she always disliked and she wondered if a measure of suspicion had been added. She suddenly wished that she had not been foolish enough to question him on the subject of the painting he had removed which, she remembered, was totally different from what he had described; and she wondered now if he had believed her when she said she didn't remember what the subject had been. If he hadn't, then perhaps she had been right in thinking that she had seen suspicion in those cold eyes as they stared at her. She would be more careful in future.

His mood changed and he reached across the table to touch her hand.

"It was kind of you to bring my papers that I was waiting for. I appreciate it. Many thanks." It was a slightly artificial speech and Belinda moved her hand from under his, her voice cold as she said, "I told you, I had to come in to shop at the Suq."

He gave an audible sigh. "I do wish that you were not always so — prickly with me. I never seem able to say the right thing." He paused as she remained silent, then added almost slyly, "It is almost as if you — well — disliked me. I hope that is not so."

Belinda stood up, the movement so abrupt that the cup rattled in the saucer on the table. For some reason, she felt as if the words were a threat and the silence was a long one, until she said quietly, "Aren't you letting your imagination run away with you?" Turning from the table, she started moving towards the house.

"Belinda."

He hadn't raised his voice but the word brought Belinda to a halt although she did not turn.

"My dear, I am sorry if I have said anything to offend you." He moved to stand in front of her as he continued, "Believe me, that is my last wish."

He made no move to touch her but she felt compelled to look at him. He smiled as he said in his pleasant voice, "You are a very attractive girl whom I have aways admired. Please believe me when I say that I would be very distressed if any harm came to you through me."

Surprised at the sincerity and choice of words, Belinda said coolly, "Why should any harm come to me?"

At her words, his mood changed again and he turned towards the house saying with a shrug, "Yes, indeed — why should it?" He offered her a small smile as he moved forward. "I mustn't keep you any longer. You will want to do your marketing before it is too hot." In the hall, he thanked her again for bringing the papers and took his leave as if they had just had an ordinary conversation, but as she drove away Belinda had the feeling that she had just received some sort of warning.

11

ALTHOUGH she still felt shaky, Belinda was reasonably satisfied with what she had achieved and, when she told Richard, he said with some excitement, "So, you were right and there *is* some connection. What was Randal's reaction when he knew you had seen that the painting had gone?"

"He didn't panic; said the light hadn't been right and he had been meaning to change it. So I asked what had been there before."

"And he told you that it had been a desert scene? You're quite certain that it wasn't?"

"Certain. I can't prove it, but I know it was a sea painting." Silent for a moment, she added, "We know now there *is* a connection and that he intends involving Christian in such a way that if anything goes wrong *he* will appear guilty while Randal remains innocent. Quite simple, but very effective."

Richard said quietly, "I can see that I was wrong about Randal. One or two things — " he said vaguely. "And now, this." Standing up, he said, "I'm late, I must go."

It was not until early evening that Belinda walked down to the shore, wanting to see what progress had been made on the almost half-finished ship. When she saw it, she drew a quick breath. The lovely lines were becoming visible and suddenly she decided to climb on board. Reaching the ladder, she climbed to the deck, carefully picking her way through a tangle of timbers.

A sharp sound startled her and she froze. Someone moved above her and she saw him, standing watching her. He was smiling. "I'd no idea you were so interested in the ship."

Belinda pulled herself together quickly.

"It's come on so much since I was away. I wanted to have a look — I thought there would be more to see." She wondered why she was bothering to explain. He started climbing down towards her. "Were you looking for anything special? Something you wanted to see?" he asked as he reached her, and she was aware of those cold eyes regarding her with amusement. The absurdity of meeting Randal Kent under these circumstances suddenly struck Belinda as funny and the thought restored her confidence.

"What a ridiculous place to meet," she commented, not answering his question and he frowned.

"What did you expect to find?" he persisted and she suddenly realized that his question had been serious, that he was genuinely suspicious of her; that he really thought that she had come on a fact-finding mission. He must be getting jittery about his built-in hiding places. He was still waiting for her reply and she said lightly, "I don't know exactly — general interest mostly, cabins, perhaps. I don't know anything about shipbuilding." She paused, then couldn't resist adding, "Perhaps I hoped to find something exciting."

He looked at her with a puzzled expression saying, "I find you difficult to understand; to know when you are serious — to know what your ideas are."

Smiling, she asked, "Why should my ideas bother you?" And turned away to leave the ship and was slightly daunted when she was confronted by the angle of the ladder down which she had to climb. It had seemed quite easy coming up, and she had no wish to fall off while this man stood watching her. As she hesitated, he enquired politely if she needed any help. She shook her head and, taking it slowly, arrived at the bottom without mishap, starting at once to walk away but heard his voice behind her.

"In answer to your question, I don't know why your ideas should bother me, but as I said, I find you difficult to understand."

"How fortunate then, that there *is* no need for you to do so."

It was nearly dark now as they walked together and for a few moments Randal was silent, then he said slowly, "It is always better to understand than to misunderstand, for that can be dangerous."

Belinda didn't answer but once again felt uneasy. Suddenly, he stopped, standing in front of her. "I must leave you here. I've left my car on the road above." He made no effort to leave her but after a moment said quietly, "Keep to what you know and understand. You are a sensible girl — don't get mixed up in other people's business. Remember what I am saying. And now — good night."

Without giving her time to reply, he turned and walked quickly up the sands to the road.

She stood where he had left her, watching him disappear into the night and, in spite of the hot air, suddenly she shivered. Once again, he had warned her; once again, he had made her afraid. It was not until she heard the car engine, that she continued walking along the sands.

She experienced a sense of relief when she saw the light shining from the house and was instantly annoyed with her own reaction to what Randal had said. She had never felt like this before. She was behaving stupidly. Randal had not even touched her; had not even raised his voice; had done nothing to make her afraid. Rather what he had said should have reassured her. It had merely been a warning. A warning against what? She walked slowly up to the house, glad to see that Richard was sitting reading. He looked completely relaxed as he put down his book when he saw her.

"Cooler now. Did you enjoy your walk?" He turned to look at her, then asked sharply, "Anything wrong?"

"No, not really. I went to have a look

at the dhow, to see what they had done while I was away."

"They've done wonders. You must have seen a big change in her."

She sat in the chair facing him, aware of an absurd relief that she was home, aware too, that she was behaving stupidly. She made an effort to speak calmly as she answered Richard.

"Yes, I was surprised. I climbed up inside — I mean on deck." She paused, then added, "Randal was there."

Frowning, he asked, "Doing what?"

She shook her head, "Nothing as far as I could see. I suddenly felt that someone was watching me. I was standing on the deck after climbing up the ladder and he was standing above me — I suppose where they are building the cabins. At first, he seemed amused, then he asked me if I was looking for anything special."

"And?"

"I don't think I answered that. I said something about it being an absurd place to meet and he asked me what

I expected to find and I said I didn't know."

"Did he seem suspicious?"

"Not *really* suspicious, and I think I managed to put him off."

She pressed her fingers against her eyes as if that would clear the scene for her. Richard said reasonably, "There is no reason why he should be suspicious of *you*. He can't have any idea that we know about the hiding places on the ship. If it hadn't been for the accident to Hassan's son, we shouldn't have known anything about it. Hassan was doubtless being paid well to keep quiet."

"Yes, it's fortunate that gratitude for his son's life changed his loyalties and I am sure we can rely on Hassan now he has made up his mind."

They talked a while longer then Richard finally said, "Don't worry too much. I can't see why you should be in any danger. Given the fact that Randal is not aware that we know what he has arranged with Hassan, it can only be guilty conscience which is making him so jittery. That and the photograph in the newspaper, which has undermined his confidence to some extent; but he is not new to this game I'm sure and his risks are spread widely and he must feel pretty certain that he has got everything possible covered without risk to himself even if things did go wrong."

"Are you saying that nothing can be done to stop him getting away with this?"

For an instant, Richard didn't answer, then he said slowly, "I don't think he *will* get away with it but *we* can't do anything except wait for developments."

"Then, who *is* doing anything to stop him? The English police didn't seem very interested." Belinda sounded angry and for the first time Richard smiled. "Don't be too sure of that."

She turned to look at him. "Do you mean that you know something?"

As he moved across the room, he said quietly, "Not very much — only enough to be sure that the police have taken this seriously and that there is nothing we can do at the moment."

She followed him to the door, saying impatiently, "If you know something, why can't you tell me?"

"I only know what I've just told you. There is nothing either of us can do which will alter what is happening. Just go on as usual — don't let Randal think anything has changed or that you are suspicious of him or know anything detrimental to him. Do that and I am sure you need not worry, so good night."

She stared after him as he continued on his way to his bedroom, feeling that she was watching a stranger. The speech he had just made was entirely out of character but she knew her brother well enough to be sure that she would get nothing more out of him.

12

IN England, although improving, Christian was not yet ready to return to Oman. Since Belinda had found the newspaper photograph, he had been worried and he finally told Benedict that he should tell the police of his own knowledge. He was surprised at Benedict's reaction.

"I hoped you'd say that — it will be unpleasant for you."

"But, I can't live with things as they are. Perhaps the police will not be interested."

It was, however, the sort of lead they had been waiting for and were keen to hear every detail. A bale of material destined for Oman and for which Randal was the agent, had brought to light a hidden painting. So, now they had a definite connection.

"You still want to go through with

your part as planned?" Benedict asked.

Christian smiled. "Very much so. I'd like to be there when they catch him."

Benedict said sharply, "You must realize that you are mixed up in something extremely serious — owing to your own foolishness. The only thing we are clear about is that Randal has planned this carefully so that if there *is* a slip up, it is you who will be caught while he remains innocent."

Christian moved, and winced. "A grand notion until that photograph. If Belinda *is* right, then that has really messed up his plans."

"I wish Belinda would keep out of this. She may have made Randal suspicious."

"It won't be too long now before I can go back. I'll keep a watch out for her."

"Yes, I know that but — " Benedict stopped short, staring at Christian.

"I wonder," he said suddenly.

"You wonder what?" Christian asked,

and then, for the next ten minutes listened carefully.

It was about a week later that Belinda waited at the airport to meet Christian.

"I didn't expect to see *you* here tonight."

The voice behind her was both unexpected and unwelcome. She turned slowly, saying, "You too, are meeting someone?"

"No, I've been signing documents for some imports and, as I was leaving, I saw you waiting." Nodding towards the barrier, Randal said, "I didn't know Christian was well enough to come."

Belinda didn't answer, her eyes on the limping figure making a slow approach, and saying, "Quite a welcome, I didn't expect to see *you* Randal."

"Quite by chance, I'm afraid. I saw Belinda just as I was leaving. How are you? It's good to have you back."

"Better, thanks," and then, turning to Belinda said, "Thanks for coming. Benedict sent his love but he won't be out just yet. Business is looking up. We've been quite busy."

Belinda asked, "Have you to wait for luggage?"

"No, I left everything I need at the apartment."

"Then, let's leave." She turned abruptly, walking away with Christian limping behind her.

When they reached the car-park she flung herself into the driving seat in silence, watching him open the other door, climb in and set his stick carefully down beside him.

"You don't need that, do you?"

His eyes were amused as he met her furious stare. "It was quite a moment, wasn't it?"

"Don't ever do anything like that to me again."

"I had no idea that Randal would be there." He leaned across in an attempt to kiss her but she pulled away impatiently. "I suggest that you keep up your charade in case Randal comes into the car-park."

In silence she started the engine and he said, "I'm sorry, I didn't mean to make you angry. Why are you so upset?"

They reached the road before she said, "What would you have done if I had given the game away?"

"Fortunately I saw you in time. Certainly the whole point would have been lost."

"What is the point?"

She was driving fast along the coast road and he said, "Look, find somewhere to park and I'll try to explain."

Silently she drove on until they reached a long stretch of empty road and she brought the car to a standstill, sitting slumped back in her seat waiting for him to speak. He said, "I've never seen you angry like this."

"What an irritating thing to say."

She heard him sigh. "How could I know that Randal was going to be at the airport? Surely you can see that?"

"Of course I can see that, but it

still doesn't make sense. I can't see any point in your pretending to be Christian."

"Listen, and I'll try to explain. You know we contacted Patrick and drew a blank?" She nodded and he continued, "Later, he rang me to tell me he had heard what he called a snippet which he thought might interest us."

Belinda threw him a withering glance. "It must have been quite a snippet to induce you to impersonate your brother."

He reached across to grip her hand, continuing to hold it as he went on seriously, "Yes, it was, for the first time Randal's honesty seemed to be in question and, from what Patrick said, in a way which seemed to connect up with what we already know."

"So — what did you do? What about Christian?"

We talked it over pretty thoroughly and he agreed that we couldn't just stay silent, so I contacted the police who were of the opinion that there *may* be a connection."

After a silence, she said, "So where does this play-acting come in? I can't see any point."

"That was my idea because Christian is not ready to come out yet and it is becoming obvious that if Randal has a plan, it must be carried out as quickly as possible, and of course, with no risk to himself."

"You mean because Christian is to take all the risks?"

"Exactly. The whole success of Randal's plan is its simplicity. Even so, he seems to have slipped up on the bales of material though the risks are pretty well spread out with nothing directly connected to him."

Belinda said, "Randal must still be taking *some* risks however careful he is."

Benedict gave a short laugh. "Yes, of course. You can't embark on something of this size without taking *any* risks. What he is doing is reducing those risks to a minimum, using people of unblemished character to do his dirty work. Not difficult if you can find someone like Christian who had got himself in a fix." He stopped speaking for a moment before saying, "The building of the dhow must have been a godsend. That will make it all a lot easier."

She said bitterly, "With you taking all the risks. Is that why you switched with Christian?"

"That was *not* the reason." He sounded angry. "It was not Christian's wish that I should do it."

"Then — why?"

"Because we don't want any change in Randal's timing and it is impossible for Christian to carry out his part yet."

"And, if he is not fit enough for the first voyage?"

Benedict said shortly, "He will be. He just needs more time." He moved his hand from hers as he said, "Don't ever make the mistake of thinking that Christian is a coward. I had great difficulty in making him agree to me coming."

There was a silence before she said quietly, "I'm sorry. I didn't mean to imply that but — I don't want either of you to get hurt."

His expression changed and he smiled saying, "I'm glad about that anyway."

She leaned forward to start the engine. "We'd better go. Tell me the rest at home — Christian. It isn't going to be easy to call you that."

"It won't be complete disaster if you or Richard make a mistake; as twins, we are quite used to being called the wrong names. So, don't worry too much."

13

BELINDA watched her brother carefully as he greeted Benedict, saw him accept him in his new character without hesitation and she gave a sigh of relief. If Richard accepted the deception, there was little chance of anyone detecting it. She felt tired and confused with too much happening at once. Looking at Richard, she said flatly, "It is not Christian."

He turned to the man still standing holding his stick, studying him carefully. Shaking his head, he said, "I'll take your word for it. I imagine there must be an adequate reason for this. It had better be good."

Abandoning his support, Benedict sat down. "I am afraid it is all becoming too complicated. Let me try to explain, starting with the phone call from Patrick which finally decided Christian and myself that we should tell the police what we know."

"What was their reaction?"

"They didn't exactly go overboard with joy. What we had to tell them was not very definite. We couldn't prove what we were saying and if it hadn't been for Belinda recognizing that photograph of the painting, I doubt if they would have been very impressed."

"And now?" Richard asked.

"Now, if they discover any further paintings hidden in bales of cloth, they will believe that we do have a connection with all of this. This case is on a big scale and they want to deal with it in a complete way." He smiled at them. "Everything is in a low key and the police want to keep it that way until they are ready." After a moment, he continued. "They realize that Christian's part is not only to deliver the goods, but also to cover for Randal, and because of that, we make no move, everything remaining the same here. We do nothing except that they would like to know the hiding place on the ship."

Belinda looking thoughtful, said, "We too want to know that, so — "

Richard interrupted, "What have you in mind?"

"We have to find out ourselves."

"What are you proposing?"

She smiled broadly. "A private visit to the ship when no one else is there."

Benedict said gloomily, "Isn't that a waste of time?"

Belinda shook her head. "I don't think so. I've a good idea where it will be, but the only way to find out is to look."

"And you intend to do that." It was a statement.

Belinda said smilingly, "You don't have to come. If you don't care for the idea, I'll go alone."

"Don't be daft — you'd break a leg or do something silly. You don't go at all unless I go with you."

It was after midnight when two darkly

clad figures set out along the sands, walking silently, moving cautiously towards the ship. As their eyes became accustomed to the darkness, a faint outline loomed ahead of them.

It was a long climb in the dark and not easy but as they reached the deck the moon broke through the clouds and Benedict turned on a small torch and they made their way along a deck crowded with timbers and ropes.

"Why such a small torch?" Belinda asked having tripped over a rope.

"Because I don't want any light to show from outside."

"Surely you don't expect anyone to be watching at this hour, do you?"

"Perhaps not, but it wouldn't surprise me."

A rough ladder took them down to a lower level and Belinda was conscious of the scent of wood. She followed close behind Benedict as he moved forward and, after a few minutes, he shone his torch into a large open space.

"This will be the luggage hold and according to Hassan is where the extra space has been made." The torch came to rest on what looked like a row of cupboards, each with a lock and number. "For the passengers to lock up their valuables," Benedict said as he swung one door open and shone the torch inside, running a finger round the smooth back of the compartment feeling for any join in the timber, but he could find no sign of any opening and moved to the next compartment doing the same. Then he stopped abruptly, laid his hand firmly on Belinda's arm and switched off the torch. After a moment, he murmured to Belinda to stay put, saying he wanted to look around. At first, she could hear nothing, then came the sound of a footstep overhead. She heard Benedict move away into the darkness beyond and was annoyed to find that she was trembling as she listened for any further sound. At first there was nothing, then she became aware of a faint shuffling coming nearer. Benedict? No. Every muscle was tense as she waited. Her eyes, more accustomed to the darkness now, saw a movement and she drew in a breath to scream. The next second a hand clamped itself across her mouth and for the first seconds she struggled, then forced herself to think more clearly suddenly aware of the familiar scent of aftershave. Behind his hand she struggled to say his name, and then he took his hand away, saying under his breath, "Don't make any noise, don't move." And then he was gone, almost without a sound.

Belinda remained where she was, her mind in a whirl. What was Slade doing here? What was his part in this? Did she know that Benedict was with her? Had he seen him? Was Benedict all right? Where was Slade now?

A few minutes later, she heard voices above her and felt herself relax as she recognized both Slade's and Benedict's. Remembering what they had come for, she moved round in the restricted space feeling round with a hand at the back of the compartment, came on a slight indentation and felt the wood move and was aware of sudden excitement. At the same time, she heard the two men returning down the ladder, making no attempt at silence. She heard Slade laugh and was on the point of calling out to tell them of her find, then suddenly decided against it as she realized that Slade did not know Benedict's identity, remembering in time her promise to Benedict not to divulge it. She heard Benedict say, "I told Belinda to stay put in one of the luggage compartments until I discovered who was here."

Slade answered easily, "Yes, I know — we met — I thought I'd caught someone."

Benedict said quickly, "Poor girl, she must have been frightened."

They had almost reached her as Slade said calmly, "Oh, I don't think so. I fancy she recognized me."

"In the dark?" Benedict's voice was

sharp and, as she left the compartment to join them, she said with some amusement, "Yes, I recognized his aftershave." And she couldn't suppress a smile when she saw Benedict's expression.

Slade shone his own torch round the space she had just left. "These are the places for luggage you mentioned — large enough to lock up their goodies." He didn't seem very interested and Belinda asked, "You've not seen them before?"

"Only on Christian's plan."

"Is that why you came tonight?"

"No. I saw a light and came to investigate."

"Well — have you — " Belinda began but Benedict broke in saying, "You are ready to go now, aren't you?" And there was something in his voice which made her agree at once although she had been going to ask Slade's opinion of what they had seen, but now she followed them to the ladder and climbed up on to the deck.

They left the ship together but separated as soon as they reached the shore, Slade going in the opposite direction. As they continued along the sands, Belinda asked, "Why did you hurry me away?"

At first, he didn't answer, then said slowly, "When I spoke to the English police, they made it very clear that they did not want any amateur interference in any form from anyone — which obviously includes us."

"So, you have decided not to trust Slade. That's it, isn't it?"

"It's hardly a question of trust, but of keeping the whole thing as quiet as possible and giving the police the chance of doing their work as well as they can without any interference." He seemed irritated. "You are being a bit childish, aren't you?"

"Well, you don't like him, do you?"

Suddenly he laughed, stopped and took her in his arms, kissing her fiercely.

Leaning against him, her own mood

changing, she said, "You didn't like the aftershave bit, did you?"

Smiling, he said frankly, "Well — not awfully."

She turned quickly, holding his face between her hands. "Stop being silly. You don't have to worry, but don't forget, I've known Slade a long time and we've always been good friends. *Only* good friends," she added, looking up at him. "It's just that — well — I should hate you to think that he would ever take part in anything crooked." Then, moving away from him, she added brightly, "Besides, why would he want to, anyway? There'd be no point." Then, pushing her arm through his said, "Come on, let's go home. Half the night's gone already."

Before he finally left her at the house, he asked her a question. "Can you remember if at any point you called me Benedict?"

There was a pause before she answered thoughtfully, "I very nearly did in those first moments — but — no,

I'm sure I didn't. I didn't say either name. It was only a couple of minutes before he went off to find you — and I heard him call you Christian." She glanced sharply at him in the hall light she had just switched on. "Why would it matter Slade knowing?"

He said quietly, "We don't want any complications at this stage, so be careful."

"Yes, I suppose you are right. All right, I'll be careful."

14

BELINDA hadn't been able to sleep, her mind still dealing with the problems of last night. Obviously Benedict was still suspicious of Slade and although she didn't believe that he was working with Randal, she was still not entirely satisfied with his explanation for being on the ship. With her own feeling of possible doubt, came a sense of guilt and disloyalty to Slade.

At breakfast, Richard wanted to know more about their midnight visit and showed surprise at the meeting with Slade.

"He'd seen lights and thought he'd better investigate," Belinda said, adding, "Benedict is suspicious of him."

"Of *Slade*? Why?"

"Benedict thinks he knows a lot more about all this than he admits."

"And you?"

She wanted definitely to refute the idea. Instead, she hesitated before saying slowly, "I can't believe that Slade is connected with anything that Randal is doing but — "

"But what?" Richard asked sharply.

She shrugged. "Oh Richard, I don't know. Benedict says he seems interested in everything Randal does — almost as if he is watching him."

"If Benedict is suspicious of him, why doesn't he speak to him?"

"The police don't want us to get involved."

There was a silence before Richard said, "You know Slade better than any of us — do *you* feel he is involved in anything?"

She poured more coffee for him, saying thoughtfully, "You know, I have to be careful about talking to Slade because Benedict is so absurdly jealous of him — well, Slade has been preoccupied and somehow — anxious lately. I hadn't thought it had any connection with Randal though."

Richard gave a short laugh. "I think you are saying that you thought it might be to do with you. You and Benedict."

"I did wonder," Belinda said, looking embarrassed. "But, not any more. After last night I am certain that there is something else that he is worried about." She stopped. "Benedict thinks it is Randal, but I can't believe it." She gave a rueful smile. "Going back to jealousy because I tend to defend Slade."

Richard said, "The simple solution is to ask Slade outright."

"You think he would listen?" she asked.

"To you? Yes, I'm sure he would."

"Is it important?"

"It could be very important, yes."

"All right. I'll do it today."

Two hours later, she heard that Slade had left Oman for England. She thought it odd that he had not mentioned it until Richard told her that he had had an emergency call from his father but would be returning soon.

In the meantime, work on the dhow increased its tempo as the date of the cruise came closer. Only Hassan remained calm and certain that the ship would be ready on time.

Ten days later, Benedict met Christian at the airport and on the drive back brought him up to date with the work which had been done.

"Are you certain you are fit enough to do this?"

Christian smiled saying briefly, "Try to stop me. This is my big moment."

"What about the English police?"

"They seem to be well advanced and all the time they are working with the police here and they seem satisfied that Randal is still unaware of their interest."

It was not until the ship was on her way from Sür to Matrah that Christian met Randal again and in a jubilant mood.

"Wonderful — everything finished

on time," he told him, as if the whole project had been his own.

The cruise was fully booked and officially commenced from Matrah harbour the following day after a dinner dance at the Gulf Hotel in Muscat.

There was a small crowd to watch the dhow sail into Matrah harbour on her arrival and Christian drew a deep breath of pleasure at the sight. Beside him, Benedict said quietly, "Congratulations, you've done it." And that was the moment Christian realized that his dream had come true.

Randal watched the brothers, annoyed as usual that he could not recognize them individually. It destroyed his sense of power. He would be relieved when Christian was finally aboard. Only then could he be certain that he was dealing with the right brother.

Richard had told Belinda that Slade had returned but they did not meet again until he joined them at dinner that night when she reminded herself that she needed to talk to him. Obviously it could not be now, but she hoped for an opportunity later. Perhaps at the dance.

The band was excellent, and there was no shortage of dancers, among them, members of the cruise.

Entering the room, Belinda turned at the sound of Slade's voice. "Let's dance." And at once, he swept her into the dance rhythm and it was a moment before she asked, "Was it all right for you in England?"

He took his time to answer, then said, "I hope I've sorted things out."

"I'm sorry. Is there anything I can do?"

"Nothing except to keep out of this." His voice was harsh.

"Out of what? I know there is something wrong. Oh Slade, please tell me."

Abruptly, he stopped dancing, leading her out into the dark garden to a balustrade on which he leaned before saying angrily, "All I want is for you to keep out of this. You can't do anything."

Leaning beside him, she said, quietly, "We have known each other a long time and I really need to know. Please don't be angry. I think you are — " She hesitated then finished in a rush, "I am so afraid you are mixed up in something serious — something dangerous."

"What are you saying? What do you mean?"

"Randal. It's *who* I mean," and when he remained silent she said urgently, "We *must* talk."

He said bitterly, "You too? I know Benedict doesn't trust me."

"Because he doesn't understand. Please tell me — where do you come into this?"

"I don't fit into it. That's the trouble."

"The trouble?"

He nodded, saying, "Yes, Randal is an old friend of my father's. A friendship which goes back a long way."

"How can it affect anything here?"

"It is a long story. It began for me when I overheard a phone call between my father and Randal some time ago when I was in England."

He was silent for so long that finally she said, "Please tell me — it's important."

He took a deep breath, saying, "It's not easy because I don't know all the answers. My father, as you know, is an antique dealer in a fairly big way, and over the years, Randal has put quite a lot of business his way. It was not until I heard them talking on the phone in England that it ever occurred to me to have any doubts about — " he hesitated, then continued harshly, "about dishonesty."

"Slade — I'm so sorry. You must have been terribly worried. What did you hear?"

"It was after one of the big burglaries and Randal was asking my father about the value of some of the paintings which had been reported stolen." He stopped and she went to lean on the balustrade beside him, aware that he was finding this very difficult.

"I'm almost certain that that was the first time my father realized that Randal was in any way connected with these burglaries, but from then on he was a very worried man. Because of that and what I'd heard on the phone, I began to watch Randal, both here and when we happened to be in England at the same time." He stopped abruptly, taking his hands from the balustrade saying, "The rest, you know."

After a silence during which Belinda's mind raced, Slade asked suddenly, "What about Christian? Randal involved him, didn't he?"

"Yes. He used him."

"So — what happens now? Is he in trouble? I've been holding hard in case anything I did made it worse for him."

"Christian will be all right. I can't tell you any more yet but it will work out now and — well — thank you for thinking about him."

Slade said, "You didn't trust me, did you?"

"Oh Slade — I'm sorry. I didn't know what to think. You seemed to know so much — and then — that business on the ship. I've been so worried."

He said a trifle bitterly, "Oh, I see how it could happen, but that part has been pretty rotten. I am glad that it is over, but please, still be careful. This is the most dangerous stage for Randal, and he can't afford for anything to go wrong now."

Other people were now coming out into the gardens and they were joined by Christian and Benedict. Conversation was general and concerned with the commencement of the cruise the following day.

15

AFTER joining the others, Belinda had no chance of talking to Slade. As they reached the hotel, bending close, he said in her ear, "Keep this to yourself." At that moment, she was very aware that Benedict was watching Slade and although he could not have heard the words, his expression showed clearly his distaste of what must have looked like a confidence. She had had every intention of giving Benedict Slade's news, hoping that it would change his attitude. Now she could not do this. She did not doubt Slade and his anxiety for his father's apparent involvement with Randal, nor his obvious hatred of the man. Slade's insistence on her own safety had surprised her, but now she recollected uncomfortably those moments the first time she visited the ship when she had felt herself watched and had looked up to see Randal standing there above her; she remembered the stab of fear which ran through her. Reaching the hotel she stood for a moment by the window. The band was playing the final dance and already people were thinning out. The twins were standing at the other end of the room and, as soon as they saw her, Benedict came across and asked at once, "Did you find out anything from Slade? What was he telling you as you came in?"

She had had no time to plan what she would say and now hesitated and, at her hesitation, saw the anger in his eyes. For a moment she was tempted to ignore Slade's request. Before she could answer, his voice sarcastic, he said, "Discussing old times, was he?"

She stared at him before turning away, saying, "He was talking to me about his father."

"Must have been interesting. You looked very intrigued."

Belinda was annoyed to find her

eyes filling with tears. "You are being absurd, allowing stupid jealousy to take over. You don't need to be jealous of anyone — it's you I love and want to marry but please remember that Slade and I have been friends for years and are fond of each other. If you trust me, you have to accept that without this awful jealousy. I know that you don't trust *him*." She stopped, overtaken by split loyalties, wanting to do what Slade had asked her yet needing to explain to Benedict to end the anger between them. She said helplessly, "Oh darling. Please try to understand. I am certain now that we can trust Slade — he hates Randal and his interest in all this is because he is worried about his father. Please believe it."

He came to her then, putting his arms round her, but she pulled away from him saying, "It's quite simple, Slade asked me not to mention what he told me so I've not done so. What he told me has convinced me that he has good reason to hate Randal."

"You sound very sure of Slade. I only hope he is not taking you for a ride. I am sorry that you are so angry with me. Perhaps it is silly to be jealous, but I love you so much and I still find it difficult to believe that you love me."

She turned to him impulsively, her anger dying. "Oh Benedict, don't let us quarrel. I hate this. I will ask Slade if he will let me tell you, or if he will do so himself."

Drawing her against him, he said gently, "Very well, ask him — but suppose he won't — what then?"

"He will. He is trying to protect his father. He will explain and I feel sure you will understand and feel as I do."

He bent to kiss her saying, "This all means so much to Christian; nothing must spoil it now." At that moment, Christian came through the hall and joined them saying, "We've an early start in the morning. I'm off to bed." Turning to Belinda, he asked, "Shall I see you then?"

"Yes, of course, I wouldn't miss it for anything."

"Are you going aboard tonight?"

"Yes, and I have just received instructions from our friend."

Benedict asked quickly, "What did he say?"

Christian grinned. "He obviously thought I was expecting to be given a parcel for delivery. Instead, he handed me a key and explained the existence of the hidden cupboard. He said all I had to do was to go to the number ten luggage compartment using my own key, then press a knob in the back panel which will slide back and take out a package I will find there. Someone will contact me as I leave the ship." He finished with a smile, "And, believe it or not, that is all I have to do. Cloak and dagger stuff on a small scale."

"So, he must have placed the paintings there earlier knowing that they would be quite safe." That was Benedict, who added with some relief, "So he is evidently beginning to relax."

"I still think he is not certain it is Christian who is sailing."

"But at this late date, it surely can't make much difference. He evidently feels safe enough with only the delivery to be made."

They walked down to the harbour with Christian who seemed cheerful and, as they reached the ship, Belinda said quietly, "This is a dream come true isn't it? Don't let all this spoil it for you. Savour every minute."

"Yes, I shall. Few things come in this world without payment and whatever I am paying for this won't be too much."

When they left him, he was looking pleased and excited and they walked back to the hotel arm in arm feeling far more relaxed with each other.

When Belinda left Benedict as she reached the hall, Slade was picking up his room key at the desk, and she waited for him to come across to her.

"Slade, I want to talk to you — to

135

ask you something."

For a moment, he stood looking down at her, then said quietly, "Something worrying you? Something I can help with?"

"Only if you want to. You don't *have* to."

Taking her arm, he steered her out of the open door to the gardens. He said, "Now relax. Tell me what the trouble is."

One part of her was relieved that he was making it easy, but she was still finding it difficult to explain why she was asking him to release her from her promise. Finally she rushed in without further thought.

"Benedict didn't — " She stopped abruptly, not sure what she had been going to say and Slade said calmly, "Benedict didn't like me talking to you. He was jealous. Is that right?"

"Yes. But how did you know?"

"I've watched him. It wasn't too difficult to work out. So, what happened?"

"He wanted to know what we were talking about, and of course, I couldn't tell him, and that made it worse."

"Yes, it would; so now," he paused, finishing slowly, "I think you are asking me to tell him what I told you."

"Yes."

"But he doesn't trust me, does he? He thinks I am working for Randal."

"Not any more. What I told him was that your interest was entirely different and that you hated him."

"No doubt his reaction was to think I was taking you for a ride."

She couldn't resist a smile at hearing Benedict's exact words but she said quickly, "Won't you please let me tell him — or tell him yourself? He would believe you and understand about your father. Surely it would be better for us to work together and help each other."

He was silent a long time, then he said slowly, "How certain are you that he would believe me?"

"Quite certain. I know what he would

feel if it were his own father. Oh Slade — just talk to him. You will know then how worried he is for Christian." Again he let the silence lengthen and it was Belinda who broke it, asking, "Why is it so important that I shouldn't mention what you told me?"

"Firstly because I knew he didn't trust me, then because — my father means a lot to me and he and Randal have been friends for years. This came as a terrible shock for him."

"Is that why you went to England?"

"Yes. I had to know how closely he was involved. Fortunately, I was in time to sort things out for him and that is why I am anxious for him that none of this touches him now. If his name was connected with any of this, it would affect his business. Now do you see why I didn't want it known?"

"Yes, of course, I understand. I wouldn't do anything to hurt your father. Oh Slade — Benedict wouldn't repeat anything you told him, I promise you. I do so hate Benedict being so stupidly jealous. It's horrible."

Suddenly he smiled. "It's quite normal I think, for a man in love to be jealous and Benedict is very much in love — you are lucky." His smile widened as he said, "All right I will take your word and trust him. Where *is* Benedict?"

"He came in with me, but I think he went out again."

"Don't worry, I'll find him."

From the open hall doors Belinda saw the two men meet. Too far away to hear their words but she saw Benedict point to a seat and they sat down, still talking. It was nearly half an hour before they walked back to the hotel. As they reached her Slade said at once, "It's all right. We've sorted things out, so don't worry any more. We have to be up early, I'm going to bed."

After Slade had left them, Benedict said, "You were right. He was in a difficult situation and he was playing a lone hand. Now we can work together. I'm sorry darling for being so silly."

"Just remember what I told you. Just be happy with it because you've got me for keeps."

16

THE voyage had been carefully planned with the outgoing journey sailed without interruption to Dubai where the ship would remain for two days before visiting the trading ports on the return voyage, ending the tour back at Matrah. It had been reckoned that allowing time for the passengers to enjoy the ship itself and to enable them to sample the produce of the trading ports at a leisurely pace the tour would take about a week and Belinda, Richard, Benedict and Slade were intending to drive along the coastal road to time their arrival at Dubai in good time for the exciting moment when the *Belinda* would sail into the harbour.

"The timing has to be elastic," Richard told them, "because of tides and weather but we can do our drive in six or seven hours and install ourselves in the hotel with plenty of time to spare." Richard was speaking as if this was a normal arrangement for an ordinary holiday instead of something which meant so much to them all.

"And Randal?" Belinda asked. "Do we know what he has planned?"

Benedict said shortly, "Only that he will be there."

"I suppose he is taking a risk in turning up at all."

Richard said, "He has a financial interest and it is a first for all of us; his absence would be conspicuous. I fancy he has chosen the lesser of two evils."

"But I don't think that he is entirely happy," Belinda's voice held a doubtful note but Benedict said at once, "Well, it's too late now for him to change anything, but no doubt he is feeling satisfied that he has managed to implicate Christian so successfully."

It was not until the next day that they saw Randal again, and then it was he who joined Belinda as she entered the hotel just after midday saying, jovially, "Come and have a drink with me to wish them luck." Putting a hand under her elbow, he led her to the bar. She accepted without enthusiasm and when they were settled at a small table with their drinks, he surprised her by saying, "You have known the twins a long time, haven't you?"

"Most of my life, yes. On and off, that is."

He regarded her suspiciously. "What do you mean?"

"When we were young, our parents were neighbours and we saw a lot of each other. When we grew up, for a time, we rather lost touch."

"And then?"

"Christian had been ill. He met Richard in England and he asked him to come out and stay."

"I see. And that is when you fell in love."

Belinda picked up her glass. "Why so many questions?"

He hesitated before saying, "I find it interesting to see you all together."

"Because they are so alike?"

"That is — intriguing — yes. I admit that I find it difficult to tell them apart, which is confusing."

She said amiably, "Yes, it must be. Most people find the same difficulty."

By now, she realized that his intention was to gain some confirmation that it had been Christian who had sailed to Dubai so she decided that it might be interesting to confuse the issue further without telling any direct lies. For instance, she must remind Benedict to keep up the slight limp.

"You have never had the same difficulty?"

"Oh yes — when they were small boys, it was practically impossible to tell them apart."

"Do they ever change identities?"

"Not so often now, but at school they used to stand in for each other."

She saw him frown, then he said abruptly, "I fancy you rather enjoy the idea, don't you?"

She managed an innocent smile. "Well, sometimes it can produce amusing results." There was a long silence during which he stared at her angrily. At last he said, "I find you difficult to understand — and assess."

"I seem to remember that you said something like that before."

"I will also repeat something else I have said before." He paused and she heard him sigh before he continued, "You are an extremely attractive girl and I have always admired you." Again he stopped, looking down at the glass in front of him. "You are also intelligent."

Belinda said nothing, but this man always had the power to make her feel uncomfortable and she was suddenly aware of her heartbeat as she waited for him to finish. "You know, of course, that I have many business interests out here. These, inevitably, at times become somewhat complicated. Complications which usually work out without interference, but — " he hesitated, then continued slowly, "I have the idea that for some reason you are interested in my present business and I will warn you once more to keep out of what does not concern you and which you do not understand."

There was a long silence which Belinda did nothing to break, then, looking directly at her he said very clearly, "I am genuinely fond of you and I should be very upset if any harm came to you through me. Please pay attention to what I am saying because under certain circumstances I might not be able to stop trouble for you."

Belinda stood up as he finished speaking, both hands clasping the back of her chair. "I don't know if for some reason you are trying to frighten me, but I really can't think of anything you might do that would harm me, and I believe you when you say you don't want to. So, thank you for your warning, and now goodbye."

As she turned away, he said very

quietly, "You could be hurt by the man you are in love with."

She continued to walk towards the door, not answering, knowing that he was watching her. When she reached her room she stood in front of the dressing-table mirror regarding her reflection. Although she was no longer frightened, her heart still raced. Did she look afraid? Hopefully, she thought she looked as calm as usual. Why did he have such definite suspicions of her? She tried to think back. Had she behaved any differently? Yes, of course she had. Before, when she had brought back papers for Randal, she had never delivered them herself. Mistake number one. Searching in his house for a painting which was no longer there. Certainly mistake number two when he came into the room bringing the replacement. At best, he must have been aware of her interest; at worst, he must have connected that interest with the print in the newspaper and from that, just possibly with the burglary, though not necessarily himself as the thief. He could have been a perfectly innocent buyer. She was not satisfied with that explanation but could not produce a better one. It seemed that he held her in some sort of suspicion. That being so, he must surely be having doubts about the twins. The more Belinda thought about it, the more worried she became. Although she had not been given any details, she knew that cared planning at every stage had been carried out, the culminating point being the arrest at Dubai when Christian handed over the actual paintings. Was it still possible that even as late as this Randal might be able to foil that arrest?

17

AT breakfast Randal sat at a table by himself while Belinda, Richard, Slade and Benedict shared one at the other side of the room. The four were driving to Dubai that morning. Presumably Randal would drive alone. After her talk with him Belinda was feeling apprehensive though she comforted herself with the thought that it was unlikely that Randal could have any clear idea of the extent of her knowledge.

Benedict was very quiet and she knew that his thoughts were with Christian who must himself be feeling nervous. He was now finally committed and anxiety must be clouding his joy in this trip.

Later, they met in the hall to go out to the car-park and suddenly the full seriousness of this project hit them with Belinda saying, "We've come to the crunch now. Too late to change anything. Which reminds me — there was a phone call for Randal."

"Did he take it at the desk? Could you tell if he was expecting it?" Benedict sounded worried and she shook her head.

"No, he had it put through to his room and, no, I don't think he expected it. He sounded bothered. Not surprisingly — if there *are* any difficulties, he can't get through to Christian until they land at Dubai."

"And, nor can we," Richard pointed out.

Benedict said, "This doesn't change anything for us, but the sooner we get there the better, so — let's go."

Once they left Matrah there was not much traffic and sitting in the back Belinda dozed until Slade's voice saying suddenly, "That's Randal's car", brought her wide awake.

Two cars were parked some distance away and Richard slowed down but

Benedict said quickly, "No, don't stop. One car is empty, two people in the other, one of them a girl. Something must have happened. This must be the answer to the phone call."

"And we can't warn Christian," Belinda sounded worried, and beside her Benedict said quietly, "So, let's try to think what this means."

"Someone must have alerted him that the police have shown interest this end. He may have to change his plans."

Slade sounded excited and Benedict gave a short laugh. "But that's just what he can't do until he can get in touch with Christian. And nor can we," he added with annoyance.

Belinda said slowly, "But at least we know where he is, and we can arrive at Dubai before him. It will be interesting to see what he will do."

"I rather fancy that our friend has run into trouble," Slade said with some relish.

The hotel dining-room was nearly

full when they were shown to their table, Belinda, Benedict, Richard and Slade. Looking round as he took his seat, Richard said, "No sign of Randal yet."

"But he will turn up, it's not likely that he will give up at this stage." Benedict sounded very positive.

Belinda said, "Besides, I'm certain that he feels that he has got everything tied up so that Christian gets the blame if it doesn't work smoothly for *him*."

It was not until they had nearly finished dinner that Randal walked into the dining-room to sit at a table by the window, raising a hand in greeting when he located them. Later, in the evening, he made no attempt to join them.

For some reason, Belinda was finding it impossible to relax. Something Benedict seemed aware of as he said goodnight to her in her room, saying comfortingly, "Don't worry. It will all be over in another twenty-four hours."

She smiled. "Well, I know *you* are

worrying about Christian, but there is nothing more we can do."

As he reached the door, he looked towards the bed. "If you need me, phone me."

She was so astonished that she scarcely returned his kiss and stood staring at the bedroom door after he had closed it, wondering what he meant. Far from having a comfortable effect, his words had increased her feeling of unrest and confirmed her conviction that Benedict himself was not happy at the way things were going. It was almost without surprise that she heard the tap on the door a few minutes later. Almost with relief, she opened it, expecting to see either Richard or Slade.

"I am sorry to disturb you but I have to talk to you. It won't take long, really only a question."

She hesitated long enough for him to enter the room and close the door behind him.

Her first instinct was fear, closely

followed by anger as without giving her time to speak, he went on smoothly, "I assure you, there is nothing to be afraid of. I wouldn't do anything to hurt you, but — "

"Randal, will you please go. Whatever you wish to talk about can wait until the morning. I am tired and I want to go to bed."

He raised a hand, coming further into the room. "This won't take long and it is very important to me," he continued as if she had not spoken. He smiled, as if this conversation was merely ordinary. "Just a simple question you have probably been asked many times before." He paused. "I simply want to be certain that it was Christian who sailed yesterday. I am sure you won't mind telling me that."

In the next few seconds, Belinda's brain worked overtime while her anger grew. Obviously Slade had been right in recognizing Randal's car. It was equally obvious that something had gone seriously wrong with his plans.

But what difference could it make now which of the twins delivered the paintings? She had no idea, but if it made so much difference to Randal, she was certainly not going to tell him.

"Why is it so important?"

She didn't expect an answer but the question gave her time to think.

He said impatiently, "I hope you are not going to make this difficult. It is such a very simple question."

"But one which seems to mean a lot to you. Why?"

She saw the flicker of anger in those eyes and he said very quietly, "I did warn you to stay clear of what you don't understand and isn't any of your business anyway. It seems that you did not listen and so — now I am wondering just what *your* part in this is and — "

"My part in what? What are you talking about?"

In spite of her own anger, or perhaps because of it, she found that she was almost enjoying his obvious discomfiture as she waited for his reply, which took some time coming. They had been standing facing each other but now he came towards her, placing a hand on each shoulder and she resisted the urge to move away as he stared down at her.

"What is your concern in what I am doing? Why are you so interested in the painting I changed the other day? No doubt you remember — when you brought my papers from England?"

She offered him a tight smile. "What a lot of questions."

"And your answer?" His fingers suddenly dug into her shoulders and she winced and pushed him away, moving across the room. "I don't need to answer your questions," she said calmly, "nor have I any intention of doing so, will you please go now?"

"Aren't you being rather foolish? If I am right in thinking that the twins have switched, then it is your fiancé who will suffer. I take it that you would not want that to happen. You should be grateful for my warning and because of it, be in a position to help him."

She said with a shrug, very aware of what he had just said, "Oh no, he would not want that. He is very independent. No doubt he will cope."

He stared at her in disbelief. "Are you saying that you will do nothing to save him from — " He stopped abruptly.

"From the police?" she suggested. "Is that what you mean?"

"Of course not," he said angrily. "It is simply that there has been a change of plan — a last minute change. If you can see him as soon as they dock and arrange with him not to deliver the package he is carrying, you will be keeping him out of a lot of trouble."

"On the other hand, he is quite capable of managing his own affairs, so I'm afraid he will have to take his chances without assistance from me." After a moment, she added thoughtfully, "If you need to change his orders, why can't you meet him on the ship yourself?"

He hesitated. "Because, for some reason the police are not allowing anyone on the ship except the caterers delivering food."

He turned to look at her, adding, "So now do you see how you can help him?"

She moved quietly over to the door and opened it.

"I told you, he will have to take his chances."

"You won't help?"

She shook her head, still standing by the door.

He said unbelievingly, "And that is your final word?"

"That's right. And now, good night."

She watched him walk to the door without looking at her and as soon as he reached the landing, she closed and locked it.

18

SHE leaned against the closed door, aware that she was shaking, then crossed the room to sit on the side of the bed, her hand going out to the phone. Was this what Benedict had expected? That Randal would try to use her? A minute later she heard him pick up the phone in his room.

"Are you all right?" He sounded anxious and she heard his voice with relief.

"Yes, I'm fine. Rather pleased with myself in fact. Did you think that he would come? He seems pretty sure that it is you who have gone and Christian is here. He tried to — "

He stopped her quickly. "Wait. Don't say any more. I'll be with you in a few minutes."

She said reluctantly, "Perhaps you'd better not." He may be keeping a watch to see if you do just that."

"So what?"

Suddenly, she laughed. "Don't you see? It might make him less sure which twin you are. At present he seems satisfied that it is Benedict who has taken his package, and that is why he thought I would jump at the chance of warning him not to deliver after all."

"And what was your answer to that?"

"Implied that as you were a big boy now, you usually handled your own affairs."

She heard him laugh, then ask, "He believed you?"

"Well, he had to. I refused to interfere, then said good night and chucked him out."

"Well wait for me and only open the door when you hear me knock."

"All right, but be careful."

She was conscious of relief as she put down the phone and waited for him. She opened the door as soon as she heard him and, as soon as it was closed, he took her in his arms. "Nice

160

to be sure of a welcome," he said later as they sat on the side of the bed while he listened to her description of Randal's visit without interruption. Finally Benedict said, "He must be pretty desperate to try to use you as his messenger boy. What do you think has happened?"

"I don't know but I imagine he is now aware of police interest and therefore knows that it will not be as easy as he apparently believed was possible. If he thinks you took over because of Christian's accident, he must be very worried, 'specially because he can't be certain any longer how much we know. Until then things had been going his way. He thought Christian would be easy to manage because he was worried on his own account."

Benedict watched her as she spoke. He said slowly, "Randal's original idea of using the ship was quite simple and should have worked except for sheer bad luck."

"You mean, me recognizing the

painting in the paper?"

"Yes. After that, he could no longer feel safe, didn't know how much you knew, or, what you would do."

"But why is he so worried that he thinks you have taken over?"

"Oh — that's easy." Benedict spoke positively. "He has a hold over Christian but he has nothing on me, but his plan has evidently gone wrong; he obviously needs a quick change of plan for Christian."

"In other words, Christian now needs to deliver an entirely innocent package instead of the one on board." Belinda stopped for a moment, then, "So, in fact, what he wanted me to do was to take the innocent one to Christian while the original one remained unseen, so that when the police demand to see what Christian is carrying, they will find something quite innocent."

"That's about it."

Suddenly she turned to Benedict in excitement. "But, because I've refused to help, Christian won't know anything about this. They had sailed before Randal had the phone call and when they dock here, Christian still can't know." She was silent for a moment, then continued slowly, "So that's why it was important for him to know which of you had gone."

"Of course, it had to be Christian. He had no hold over me." Benedict paused with a grin. "But unless Randal can make contact with Christian before he leaves the ship, he can do nothing."

"So," Belinda was frowning, trying to picture the scene, "Randal needs to exchange packages while Christian is still on board. How will he get round that now that no one is allowed on the ship?"

Benedict started walking round the room, hands in pockets, deep in thought while Belinda watched him silently. Benedict said as he stopped in front of her, "If we could find a method of alerting Christian, he could stay on the ship until the last minute and only bring out his package when Randal had no chance to swap it."

"Somehow we have to get a warning to him not to come on deck with the paintings as planned."

"How do we do that if we are not allowed on the ship ourselves?"

"What time do they expect to dock?"

"Between nine and ten o'clock, but to do anything at all, we have to contact him before he attempts to make a move himself or Randal sees a chance to see him."

Belinda still sat on the side of the bed, elbows on knees, hands cupping her face. Suddenly she stood up. "I've just thought of something. What's the time?"

"Just after eleven."

She shook her head, "Then I'll have to wait until the morning."

"What have you thought of?" Benedict stopped his tramping round the room to listen.

"Jane Langdon. She is with the firm which supplies the catering for the ships that come into this port. I know her very well."

"So?"

"I know that she is hoping to come down with the caterers when they bring the supplies for the return trip, because she wants to see the ship."

"What do you want her to do?"

"Deliver a letter to Christian."

Her voice sounded triumphant and Benedict stopped his wandering.

A smile spread over his face as he came and kissed her. "Clever girl," he told her. "Do you think she will do it? Are you sure she will be allowed on board?"

"Yes, I know she will — she asked specially."

They continued discussing the details for some time. Belinda said, "I'll ring her from this phone early tomorrow. I don't need to tell her anything, only that it is important that Christian gets the note at once and privately, and I'll ask her not to mention it to anybody. She will be intrigued and I know she will do it for me, and she is very reliable." For a moment, she went to lean against Benedict with her arms round him, her head on his shoulder, immense relief running through her. "Let's get the note done now so that it will be ready in the morning."

It was still very early the next morning when Belinda reached the harbour. The whole area was full of activity, lorries and vans being loaded or unloaded. Two small ships were already leaving the harbour, the chug of their engines sounding loud in the quiet morning air. Jane's blue van was not yet here and Belinda was keeping a sharp lookout for Randal. She was aware that both English and Omani police must be among the busy crowd.

Minutes later, she saw the blue van arrive, parking some distance away and she walked over to it. Almost at the same time, Randal's car swept into the parking area and a moment later, he stood looking round as if expecting someone.

She called out to Jane as she reached the van. "I thought it was your van. How are you? I've not seen you for some time." During the phone call earlier they had agreed to meet casually and, seeing Randal, Belinda was glad that they had done so. He raised a hand in greeting but otherwise betrayed no interest while Belinda joined Jane at the van. The back doors were open and under that cover, she passed the all-important letter to Jane who slipped it into her pocket. Belinda said quietly, "Many thanks. Please don't give it to anyone but Christian and contact him as soon as possible. I'm pretty sure he will be on deck."

"Don't worry, I will be careful. But don't forget you promised to tell me all about this cloak and dagger stuff later."

"I will, but don't forget to do this as quickly as you can. It really *is* important."

Jane reached into the van for a large packing case which she handed to Belinda saying, "Carry that across. It looks innocent enough." Then picked up a case for herself. The driver started unloading as the girls walked away.

And Belinda was aware that Randal watched them from a distance as they carried their cases to where the ship would dock, and by that time, a murmur was going up from the waiting crowd as they caught their first sight of the ship as she entered the harbour. In the early morning mist, she looked like a ghost ship as she came into view. Looking round her, she saw Randal was standing a short distance away, apparently no longer interested in what they were doing. Passengers were lining the deck and Belinda said quickly, "Christian is standing at the back, wearing a pale-yellow shirt and he is carrying a parcel. Take your case in that direction, hesitate as if you are not sure which way to go. That should give you the chance of passing the note. That is all you need. Good luck and thank you."

She watched the gangway put in place but nobody was allowed on board except the caterers. Jane, still clutching her case, moved in Christian's direction. Just as she reached him, the case slipped and Christian stepped forward to help her. She let out a sigh of relief. Jane had made it.

19

CHRISTIAN had been unable to sleep and was up very early. He went at once to the luggage area, unlocking number ten with his key. The hidden panel had been so skilfully constructed that even with knowledge that it was there it took him a moment to find it. It slid back silently to disclose a narrow, medium-sized brown paper package. Lifting it out, he examined it carefully but it was an ordinary parcel, looking entirely innocent. Sliding back the panel, he returned to his cabin. Now the time was here, he confessed to feeling a trifle nervous. It would be a relief when today was over.

When he was ready, he went up on deck expecting to be able to disembark immediately but found that the gangway was only just being put into place. He watched Belinda go across to the blue van to speak to Jane, whom he did not know and a few minutes later, saw the two girls come back to the ship, when Jane picked up one of the cases lying ready. Still watching, he realized that no one but the caterers were being allowed to board the ship. It suddenly hit him that something had gone wrong for Randal. Passengers had not been warned about not being allowed to come or go. The order must have been made on shore. Not quite knowing why, he watched Jane as she reached the ship and turned his way with her case. As she reached him, she let the case slip and he moved forward to help her. She said in a low voice, "Take the note I am holding under the case quickly." As soon as he felt the note, he transferred it to his palm and closed his hand on it. Jane thanked him loudly for his help and moved on at once with her case. Christian returned to his cabin with a feeling of excitement.

He opened the note quickly.

We think Randal was warned of police interest and is anxious to change his plans. He tried to get B to meet you on ship with a packet to exchange for the original. B refused, so he will now have to do this himself. At all costs hang on to the one you have and deliver as planned. We can't do any more this end.

Good luck.

Christian read it through again, aware of rising excitement. He sat down to think. So that was the reason nobody was allowed on the ship. Evidently Randal had been right about police interest, but Randal was out there waiting, his only hope now to make the exchange in time. If he succeeded, the planned arrest was useless. There was only one way to prevent that and Christian embarked on the first stage of his own plan by hiding the original package where it would be safe for a short while. Returning on deck, he

172

saw Randal pacing up and down near the gangway looking anxious. Seeing Christian he frowned angrily as he waited for him to join him.

"What the hell have you been doing? Where is it?"

"I didn't dare to bring it up," Christian informed him. "I knew that something must have gone wrong when no one was allowed on the ship. What do you want done?"

Randal hesitated, thinking quickly, still badly perturbed. It was just possible that this was a way out if handled carefully. The trouble was that he had no idea how much the police knew. He said now, "There has been a change of plan which has made last minute difficulties." Looking round carefully, he lowered his voice. "I have a similar package which you must deliver in place of the other. Where is it?"

"Quite safe." He looked at the parcel Randal was carrying. "You'd better give me that and I will put the other back in the panel. There is still time."

Having no choice, but with some reluctance, Randal handed over the package he was carrying. Christian returned quickly to the ship and his cabin. Comparing the two parcels, he saw that they were identical; retrieving the original, carrying it under his arm, he returned to the deck, joining Randal long enough for him to see what he was carrying, then walking away to the arranged meeting place. As soon as he reached it, he thought he must be mistaken. A blonde girl was waiting alone, looking anxious. When she saw him, she came forward saying crossly, "You're late. What happened to you?" She seemed unaware of two men who were now closing in on them, and the next few seconds were a trifle confused as she suddenly realized that she was being arrested. She started to protest, but they were taken to a small office and offered chairs.

"What *is* this? What is the matter?"

"It is believed that you are in possession of valuable paintings which were stolen in England."

She looked down at the innocent-looking parcel in her hand. She was recovering quickly as she said, holding out the package Christian had handed to her, "Are you suggesting that this contains valuable paintings?" She felt entirely confident as she knew what Randal had arranged.

One of the detectives turned to Christian. "Will you please open this."

The wrappings were difficult and needed a knife but finally Christian revealed a cardboard cylinder inside which were two small paintings.

They heard the girl gasp as she saw them. "But — this is wrong. This is not what I was told. I — " She continued to bluster, clearly surprised at the sight of the paintings; evidently certain that the switch had taken place.

During the next few minutes, Christian concentrated on the scene now taking place and it was not until both the girl and himself were being taken away that he looked around him and saw Randal watching from a distance as the four of them walked away. As they neared him, he deliberately stared at him with a look of triumph and Randal would have been stupid indeed if he hadn't understood what had happened. At that moment, a man bent to speak to him and then, they were both joining the other suspects. Eventually they ended up at the local police station where the two detectives officially introduced themselves. The first man was English, the second, an Omani.

The Englishman looked round the table at which they were sitting, his eyes settling on Randal.

"I understand that Mr Christian Quint agreed to deliver a package for you when the ship arrived at this port?"

"Yes, that is so." Randal agreed readily, avoiding Christian's eyes.

"What did that package contain?"

"It contained four copies of a special art magazine I had promised to obtain for a friend."

"Why did you ask Mr Quint to make the delivery?"

There was a slight hesitation before Randal answered. "Because I was not certain that I should be here at this time. As you are aware, my business is carried on both here and in England." He paused. "As a matter of fact, Mr Quint offered to carry out the delivery for me."

Christian moved sharply as the detective turned to him.

"Was there a special reason for your offer?"

"None. There was no offer. I owed Mr Kent money and since I was at that time unable to pay my debt, he suggested that I did this service for him instead and I agreed."

"You knew what you were carrying?"

"Not at that time."

The detective turned to Randal.

"Today, you handed Mr Quint a

parcel similar to this one. What was in that?"

"I've already told you — magazines."

The detective turned to Christian. "That package is now in your cabin?"

Christian nodded and the man continued, "In fact, that is the package which you hoped would save you. I am afraid that you are too late for that because the police are now in possession of enough facts to connect you with a series of burglaries in England during the last year."

Randal said quickly, "I think you are accusing the wrong man, Christian — "

"It is merely foolish to try to implicate Mr Quint at this stage. This is the end of the road for you. A case as large as this always takes time to complete but Oman has supplied the final proofs of your involvement and I now charge you with three separate robberies in England."

For the first few moments, Randal did not move, then his self-control broke as he turned to Christian.

"So — you knew. All the time you knew. You just played along — you and Belinda. How did you know? Who told you — I — "

Christian stood up, looking down at the man who had caused him so much misery.

"You were too greedy — too sure of yourself so that you underestimated other people. You did not expect that your plans could go wrong, but if they did you thought you had worked out how I could be held guilty while you got away free. But, it didn't work out like that, did it? Do you still feel that it has been worth while?" His words had been quiet but held the deep feeling he could not hide and there was silence in the room until the detective turned to Randal ordering him to come with them. Randal seemed almost surprised but got slowly to his feet, leaving with the girl and the police.

Left alone, Christian covered his eyes with his hands. Only now, when he suddenly realized that he was free, was he fully aware of the strain he had been under.

It was not until they were back at Sür in Richard's house and all together that they were able to discuss all the details and it was Belinda who pointed out something none of them had mentioned. "You know, if it hadn't been for Slade overhearing his father's conversation with Randal, the end of all this might have been entirely different and he would still be free to commit more burglaries. As it is, he is on his way to facing serious charges."

Slade said, "No, I don't think it was entirely like that. They would definitely have caught up with him through his own arrogance. He was too sure of himself and not quite clever enough to realize how much the police already knew. He had got away with so much that he became careless — particularly with my father whom he knew to be honest. He used his knowledge and thought he wouldn't question anything he told him, and that was a mistake.

It was lucky that I was there and able to help."

"It certainly speeded things up, also, the fact that right up until the end, he was not certain about the identity of the twins."

Belinda smiled at the two men now sitting side by side. Benedict said, "Yes, well, we do have our uses, but I'm glad that Christian was well enough to make the trip. At least that was a bonus after all his troubles."

"How did the police recognize the pictures which had been stolen?"

"The answer to that," Benedict told her, "is that the owners had been sensible enough to have had them photographed. And that must have come as an unpleasant surprise to Randal."

After a silence, Belinda said slowly, "Hassan contributed a lot by telling Christian about the hidden cupboard and, of course, that explains Randal's keenness to have a part in the building of the ship. No doubt he was banking on further occasions when it might be useful."

They continued talking for some time further. The twins would return to England and their boatbuilding as soon as the *Belinda* returned from her first voyage. Already bookings were being taken for the next one so it looked as if Christian's idea had been a good one and would prove a success. Richard had promised to take on the management side of the ship in Oman which made everything much easier for the twins.

After a pause, Benedict stood up, saying with evident pleasure, "If you will excuse us, Belinda and I have a small matter to discuss."

Christian said laughingly, "You don't waste much time, do you?"

"It's always a mistake to waste time," Slade said, smiling with the rest as he got up to leave. Meeting his eyes across the room, Belinda wondered suddenly if she read regret in them as he came across to her. Bending to kiss her cheek, he said under his breath, "Some of us are too slow, but I wish you great happiness in the future."

THE END

Other titles in the
Linford Romance Library:

A YOUNG MAN'S FANCY
Nancy Bell

Six people get together for reasons of their own, and the result is one of misunderstanding, suspicion and mounting tension.

THE WISDOM OF LOVE
Janey Blair

Barbie meets Louis and receives flattering proposals, but her reawakened affection for Jonah develops into an overwhelming passion.

MIRAGE IN THE MOONLIGHT
Mandy Brown

En route to an island to be secretary to a multi-millionaire, Heather's stubborn loyalty to her former flatmate plunges her into a grim hazard.

WITH SOMEBODY ELSE
Theresa Charles

Rosamond sets off for Cornwall with Hugo to meet his family, blissfully unaware of the shocks in store for her.

A SUMMER FOR STRANGERS
Claire Hamilton

Because she had lost her job, her flat and she had no money, Tabitha agreed to pose as Adam's future wife although she believed the scheme to be deceitful and cruel.

VILLA OF SINGING WATER
Angela Petron

The disquieting incidents that occurred at the Vatican and the Colosseum did not trouble Jan at first, but then they became increasingly unpleasant and alarming.

DOCTOR NAPIER'S NURSE
Pauline Ash

When cousins Midge and Derry are entered as probationer nurses on the same day but at different hospitals they agree to exchange identities.

A GIRL LIKE JULIE
Louise Ellis

Caroline absolutely adored Hugh Barrington, but then Julie Crane came into their lives. Julie was the kind of girl who attracts men without even trying.

COUNTRY DOCTOR
Paula Lindsay

When Evan Richmond bought a practice in a remote country village he did not realise that a casual encounter would lead to the loss of his heart.